CW01095752

UNFINISHED BUSINESS

UNFINISHED BUSINESS

A NOVEL

TERRY MAHER

ROBSON BOOKS

First published in Great Britain in 2003 by Robson Books,
The Chrysalis Building, Bramley Road, London W10 6SP

A member of **Chrysalis** Books plc

British Library Cataloguing in Publication Data
A catalogue record for this title is available from the British Library.

ISBN 1 86105 630 3

Typeset by FiSH Books, London
Printed in Great Britain by Creative Print & Design (Wales), Ebbw Vale

For Barbara, Nicholas, Anthony and Jeremy

'If you can meet with triumph and disaster
And treat those two imposters just the same;'

'If—' Rudyard Kipling (1910)

Principal characters

Mark Palmer – chairman of Palmer Industries Ltd
Jeremy Stephens – senior partner of Stephens Foster, Palmer's auditors
Sarah Armstrong – head of Rainbow Asset Management (RAM)
Gerald Howard – chairman of Tudor Holdings plc
Tom Curtis – *Financial Times* journalist

Other key players

Anthony Kemp – finance director of Tudor
Nigel Kendal – finance director of Palmer
Rebecca Shaw – financial PR executive
James Gordon – director of Gresham's Bank
Alan Copeland – chairman of Chiswells, merchant bankers
Paul Davis – litigation partner at Fisons, solicitors
Edward Walsh QC – leading counsel for Stephens Foster

PART ONE: THE DEAL

PROLOGUE

It was towards the end of the afternoon of the third Thursday in September when Nigel Kendal shuffled into Mark Palmer's Regent's Park office. Nigel had been the finance director of Palmer Industries for more than twenty years. Now in his early fifties, he was a grey, chain-smoking anonymous figure with ash-stained suits and down-at-heel, scuffed shoes. He gave the impression that the world had defeated him. Today, he looked even more dejected and world-weary than usual. He closed the office door and, without speaking, and without seeking the permission that he would normally have sought, sat heavily in a chair facing Mark across the square chrome and glass desk which dominated the room.

Mark, who had not long returned from a lengthy, late and heavy lunch, was making a half-hearted attempt to review some business papers while slouched towards the back of his latest-purchase Italian, white-leather chair, with his Berluti-clad feet resting on the glass-topped desk edge. He adjusted his posture and moved the papers to one side. His first thought was that Nigel was unwell, as he observed the pasty, unhealthy-looking face and the damp, dishevelled hair.

'I have something very important to tell you,' Nigel said, 'but it will help if I can smoke.' After Mark's agreement, Nigel fumbled with his matches while he lit his cigarette with visibly trembling hands. He took two deep draws on the cigarette and then resumed. 'Mark, I have a confession to make. It will not be easy for me but I do want to tell you the truth and the whole story. So, I would be

5

grateful if you would please listen to what I have to say, and try not to interrupt me until I've finished.'

Mark appeared nonplussed. He nodded and muttered, 'Go ahead. Take your time.' At which point they were interrupted by the ring of Mark's telephone. He lifted his hand to signify that Nigel should pause in his narrative while he took the inevitable call – the third of the day – from his wife, Gail.

CHAPTER ONE

Mark Palmer's family business was started by his father in the 1930s. Mark's grandparents had come to England in 1912, among the late arrivals of the major exodus from Eastern Europe. It had been towards the end of that period of mass immigration that took place between 1880 and the start of the First World War, and that resulted, by 1914, in the number of Jews in Britain growing from 30,000 to more than 300,000.

The restrictive immigration policies introduced by the British Government at the time of the Second World War meant that the figure had grown to no more than 400,000 by 1960 and, due to the reduced birth rate of an increasingly middle-class community, it has since been in decline.

At the turn of the twentieth century, however, as many as eleven ships a week had arrived at British ports, mainly from the European ports of Hamburg and Rotterdam, bringing within them many thousands of Russian, Polish and Romanian Jews. Some had been fleeing from the horrors of the pograms, but most had been seeking a more tolerant alternative to the blatant discrimination and second-class citizen status that had been their home-life in the country of their birth. And others had simply been economic migrants who had seen better opportunities in a prosperous and heavily industrialised Britain. A few had arrived in the mistaken belief that they had reached the United States of America. They were to play a beneficial, and totally disproportionate role in the future economic, academic and cultural development of their adopted country.

Mark's grandparents had arrived from Lithuania and had quickly settled in the East End of London, where there was an established community. They had only recently married, and had determined to start their new life together in a new country. They found work in the rag trade of those times, with the husband employed as a cutter, and the wife as an outworker, 'making-up' for the neighbouring manufactories.

Mark's father, David, born in 1916, left school at fourteen, as was then the custom, and joined his parents in the garment-making industry. He was a bright and resourceful boy and soon became involved in organising a number of the 'makers-up' into a group to form a more effective economic and bargaining unit. He was later able to acquire a number of sewing machines on his own account and by the start of the Second World War was in business manufacturing garments under his own name.

During his first years at school David had been found to be suffering from pulmonary tuberculosis. The disease was almost endemic at that time in the poorer areas of the inner cities and the death rate was high. David's condition, however, had been detected at an early stage by the telltale red blotches on his shins, and he had made a fairly rapid and apparently complete recovery. Nonetheless, his medical history was sufficient to keep him out of the armed forces and he was able to continue to nurture his fledgling business through the war years. The bulk of his production was converted to the manufacture of uniforms for the War Ministry and, by the end of the war, the business was much more firmly rooted and he held important licences for the supply of essential raw materials.

He married Rachel, a girl living in the same street and of a similar background, in 1939. They agreed not to have any children until the war was over. They wanted the political uncertainty to be resolved and for their finances to be on a more secure base. Mark, their first born, was part of the post-war 'baby boom'. His birth was quickly followed by the arrival, with only a short interval between them, of his two sisters. The family was then complete.

It was about this time, in the gap before the birth of the second girl to be precise, that David and Rachel moved to a new home in the leafy suburb of Golders Green. David wanted to bring up his family in a healthier environment than what he now more clearly saw as the slums of the East End of London. And he wanted to move away from the 1930s memories of Oswald Mosley's black-shirted fascist thugs marching past the front door of his parents' Whitechapel house.

Rachel kept a traditional Jewish home and David was a devout and conscientious attender at the local synagogue. The Holy Days were strictly observed, with Friday nights being especially sacrosanct. Their three children grew up understanding, without the need for any reminder, that their presence for the lighting of the candles, the prayers and all the formal rituals of their Friday family dinner, was absolutely mandatory.

David's parents spoke only Yiddish at home and David always spoke with them in their native tongue. In a concession to their new English surroundings, and in the knowledge that it would be helpful to their son in establishing himself in life, they had changed the family name to the anglicised Palmer, from the original Palezynski, shortly after David's birth. But when he moved with Rachel and his family to Golders Green, they made it clear to him that, as far as they were concerned, they were not prepared to sacrifice the relative security of their newly found East End ghetto, and that they intended to remain in Whitechapel, and stay within its narrow, crowded but comforting streets for the rest of their days.

Mark was doted on by both his parents, but particularly by his father, and was always shown preference over his resentful sisters. 'Golden Boy' and 'Gucci' were epithets that were frequently flung at their 'spoiled' brother by the two girls as they reached their teenage years. Mark was a wilful child, whose selfish and mischief-making habits made his sisters' lives a misery. He was adept at transfering the blame for his own misdemeanours on to either of his two sisters; a stratagem which was more likely to prove successful with his father than with his less gullible mother. He attended Highgate School, a minor public school in North London, where, apart from some modest success on the sports field, he achieved no distinction. His 'O' level results were disappointing and he left school at sixteen to move into the family firm.

David Palmer Ltd, as the business was then known, had found the immediate post-war years to be difficult as people everywhere sought to adapt to peacetime conditions and to the rationing, controls and austerity that were its new features. However, in the more settled period of the 1960s and 70s, the company prospered, specialising in the manufacture of branded lingerie for the newly developing high-street retailers and, with the encouragement of government grants, a new factory was built in the north of England. This soon became the main unit of production, although a presence was retained in the East End of London for sales and marketing.

David died shortly before his seventieth birthday. It seemed that the childhood tuberculosis had left a permanent legacy in the form of scar tissue on his left lung, and he suffered from poor health and severe bronchial problems for some years before his death. At the time he died, the business was profitable, highly respected and employed more than one thousand people. Mark, after a long period of barely disguised impatience, became, in his thirty-eighth year, solely responsible for the fortunes of David Palmer Ltd.

David had been an extremely indulgent father to Mark, his long-awaited first-born and his only son. This indulgence was in sharp contrast to his disciplined and dedicated approach to his business. He stood by, almost benignly, as Mark undertook his serial marriages and divorces, and began to develop a jet-set lifestyle. Mark's mother was less tolerant and was distraught by the divorce from Mark's long-time childhood sweetheart who had finally despaired of his philandering. The first marriage was the only one to be celebrated in the traditional religious manner at the synagogue. Mark had gradually distanced himself from the rituals which had been such an important part of his parents' lives and this accelerated after his father's death. As he enjoyed long holidays at his favourite resorts in Switzerland and the south of France, he no longer liked to be reminded of his family's Yiddish-speaking Lithuanian origins. To his sisters, the 'golden boy' of their childhood had been replaced by a brother whom they referred to in distaste as 'the man with the phantom foreskin'.

David had been equally complaisant with regard to Mark's peripatetic working habits, a major feature of which was his extended vacations. The one area of business which Mark had made very much his own, however, was the relationships with some of the more important customers. His particular brand of streetwise, superficial charm had gone down well with the buyers of the leading department stores and high-street fashion chains, who were easily flattered, and sales had flourished. These key accounts became the single most important source of business for David Palmer Ltd.

After his father's death, Mark sought to stamp his own identity on the business that he had inherited. He embarked on a number of new business ventures in the hope of easy money, by pursuing the then fashionable holy grail of diversification. He changed the name of the company from David Palmer Ltd to Palmer Industries Ltd, appointed himself chairman and chief executive, and established a small separate head office which, although personally convenient, was expensive. But Mark's temperament was highly volatile, which led to a manic-depressive approach to business. He would involve himself in a mad frenzy of activity and then, quickly tiring of the effort, would take off on another of his holidays. Work was an inconvenience that was to be tolerated only to ensure that his extravagant way of life could be maintained.

Mark's father had been a prudent businessman, one of his many dogmas being an aversion to debt. He had not liked banks and he had not trusted them. He would never tire of telling his long-suffering friends that, 'as soon as the banks see the slightest sign of rain, they take away your umbrella'. Mark was very different. He did not possess his father's natural caution, nor his conscientious attention to detail. And he had been quick to make friends with the banks. The new ventures, which had been financed by bank borrowings, did not succeed. For the first time, debt became a feature of the company balance sheet.

Mark's lack of prudence was not confined to his business affairs. His personal life was also characterised by financial disarray. He took a salary of £250,000 a year, and his expensive cars and an over-generous portion of his private expenses were paid for by the company. He received dividends on his shareholding in Palmer Industries although, due to the deterioration of its finances under his stewardship, these had now to be restricted; a move which had infuriated his two sisters as their father had left an equal number of shares to each of his three children. Still, he could never make ends meet. Each year he spent more than his income. The difference had come from further bank borrowings. These had already been high as a result of financing two homes and two divorce settlements. The accumulated debt was now well into seven figures. And there were still tax bills to pay.

When one gets to a certain age, one is responsible for how one looks. As V S Naipaul has written, 'You carry your life in your face'. Mark was now a little over fifty and he was no exception to that general rule. He had not worn well. His face bore all the signs of over-indulgence. He was about average height, more than a little overweight, with fleshy lips, thick, curly, dark-brown but now grey-flecked hair, heavily lidded hazel eyes underscored by dark pouches, and a large, booming, attention-seeking voice. He wore too much gold jewellery for most people's taste and, in his anxiety to be liked, sought too obviously to impress. He lived during the week in a large house in St John's Wood and his office was a ten-minute drive away, in one of Regent's Park's elegant Nash terraces.

On a bright, sunny, late March day, Mark looked, morbidly, through his second-floor office window across the park and reflected for the umpteenth time that something had to be done. His income from the business was just not enough to meet his many commitments – not least to past and present wives – and he no longer had the option of adding to his debts. In fact, his bank had made it clear to him that his borrowings must soon be reduced.

The only person who understood the nature of his financial position was Jeremy Stephens, the senior partner of the company's auditors, Stephens Foster. As he turned his fixed gaze away from the lake and the newly budding trees of the park, he asked his secretary to telephone Jeremy's office and to arrange for them to have lunch together as soon as possible.

CHAPTER TWO

Jeremy Stephens was sitting at a table amid the starched linen and shining silver of Scotts in London's Mayfair; a smartish restaurant that, despite its recent facelift, had not recovered its former glory. However, the tables were set far apart, and the service was slow, which suited the purpose of this particular occasion. Jeremy did not approve of Mark Palmer but Palmer Industries was one of Stephens Foster's largest and most long-standing clients, and an urgent request for a business lunch was treated as if it were a royal summons. Small firms such as Jeremy's could not run the risk of offending important clients when the competition from the newly enlarged accounting firms was so intense. Jeremy had re-arranged his diary to accommodate Mark's wishes, and was now awaiting his arrival. Suddenly, in his usual flamboyant manner, Mark materialised beside the lunch table. 'Sorry to keep you waiting,' he said, loudly. 'Anyway, I'm sure that your meter is already ticking away so that it will all be on my bill.'

The convention of waiting until coffee is served before the discussion of any serious business was now rarely observed, and Mark's mood today was not one for procrastination. As soon as the food and wine were ordered, he plunged in.

'Those fucking sisters of mine,' he complained, 'and their bloody parasitic husbands. They now say that they are going to use their voting power to put one of the husbands on the board. They say that they are upset about the reduction in their dividend income. As if I'm not! It affects me just as much as it does them. But they assume that I'm being deliberately spiteful. I tell them that the business is not doing well, but they say that it's my fault and ask me what I'm doing about it. So,' he said, looking directly at Jeremy, 'you know the true state of the finances of the company, you know my own financial position and you are supposed to be the expert. You tell me what I should do. What are my options?'

Jeremy reflected ruefully that, from the tone and manner in which Mark spoke to him, it seemed almost as if he were suggesting that the mess was entirely Jeremy's fault. In seeking to answer Mark's question, he first restated the basic problem.

'The business of Palmer Industries is in need of fresh capital to replace the bank borrowings that it has accumulated as a result of the diversification policy. But an injection of new cash into the company will not, of itself, place any money into the hands of yourself and your two sisters. And, for different reasons, each of you has an urgent requirement to raise money on your own behalf. You, Mark,' he said, carefully, 'so that you can repay your debts, reduce your bank borrowings and re-establish a base from which you can finance your lifestyle. And your sisters, so that they can make up the loss of their dividend income and withdraw some of their capital from a business over which they currently have no executive control. Any solution will need to resolve both of these issues.'

At this point Mark interrupted Jeremy's measured analysis in a show of impatience. 'Surely the answer is a stock market flotation.'

'That,' said Jeremy cautiously, 'would not be easy.' There was a flurry as the waiter at last appeared with the first course and Jeremy was given a little time to collect his thoughts and to determine how to explain to Mark, as tactfully as possible, the reason for his discouraging response.

Jeremy knew that to obtain a stock market quotation, a company needs to be able to show a growth in profits over a number of years and it should also have sound and capable management that could withstand the scrutiny of the City and the financial press. Palmer Industries was a long-established and respected company. Its original core business had withstood Mark's depredations and was still extremely profitable. However, the overall profit record had been ruined by the investment in the new and now loss-making subsidiaries. And, in the City, the policy of diversification, which had been all the vogue just ten years ago, was now decidedly out of favour. The new stock market fashion was focus, and those conglomerates which had so recently been acquiring new, unrelated businesses as quickly as merchant banks could find them, were now just as quickly shedding them – often through the offices of the same merchant banks. Finally, on the management issue, the combination of Mark's autocratic style and absentee landlord habits, together with his disastrous acquisition policy, would not make the task of convincing the City that he was the right person to head a public company an easy one. Jeremy explained all of this to Mark as diplomatically as possible. His advice was that a flotation of Palmer Industries on the stock market did not seem to be a feasible option.

Mark was reluctant to accept this advice. He responded peevishly, 'I know many quoted companies that are not as profitable or as well managed as Palmer Industries.' Jeremy refrained from any immediate reply and busied himself with his food. After a gap of several minutes, Mark blurted out, 'Well, we have to do something and if it's not to be a stock market flotation, what's the alternative?'

'I believe that the only answer is a trade sale,' replied Jeremy.

'What do you mean, a trade sale?'

'Sorry,' said Jeremy, 'a trade sale is simply the sale of your business to another company, perhaps to one of your competitors, or to some expansionist company which might be seeking to diversify. There are one or two quoted conglomerates which are still acquisitive.'

Mark looked at Jeremy in dismay. 'A takeover? Fuck that! I am not bloody well going to give up my independence. We have to find some other solution. Why don't we talk to a merchant bank?'

Jeremy was not convinced that a merchant bank would be able to conjure up a more original solution to Mark's problems which, although serious, were fairly straightforward. He also felt aggrieved that his own advice and judgement were being questioned. Nonetheless, he had no alternative but to indulge Mark and agree to his suggestion. They had had dealings with the corporate finance department of one of the slightly less well-known banks on one of Palmer Industries' ill-fated acquisitions. Jeremy said that he would speak to the bank's chairman, Alan Copeland, and arrange a meeting.

CHAPTER THREE

Paul Chapman was a senior buying executive at Fraser and Green, one of the major high street retailers, which sold a wide range of household goods and clothing for men, women and children. It was known to its millions of loyal customers as 'F&G'. Mark Palmer had courted Paul over a number of years. His motive had always been to encourage the development of trading between Palmer and F&G. But what had begun as a purely business relationship had later developed into a genuine friendship. F&G had expanded rapidly over the past thirty years and was now a dominating presence in every shopping centre and on every high street. Palmers had profited from its growth and F&G was now its largest customer. It had been an essential ingredient in the continuing success of Palmer's traditional core business as manufacturers of lingerie. The benefits, however, had not just been in Palmer's direction. Paul had always driven a hard bargain on behalf of his employers and Mark had been forced to concede painfully high discounts. Still, despite the attractions of the deal which had been struck on its behalf, it would have been surprising if the board of F&G had been aware of the scale of the hospitality which Paul enjoyed at Mark's expense. The families had become close, and Paul and his wife Helen often joined Mark and his wife Gail on their holiday trips – all paid for by Mark on his company expense account. The two couples were now about to embark, before the winter season reached its end – and before Mark became involved in meetings with merchant banks – on a final long weekend's skiing expedition.

During the course of the winter, Mark would usually make four or five visits to the mountains. This time he was going to St Moritz, which was one of his favourite resorts. A problem with St Moritz, Mark had found, was that it took such a long time to get there from London. In the early years, his usual route had been to fly from Heathrow to Zurich and then to complete the journey by train. The Swiss rail service's world-renowned reputation for efficiency, good-timekeeping and comfort was well deserved, but it still took more than four-and-a-half hours to travel from Zurich airport to St Moritz, with two changes of train. It took a full day to get there and another full day to get back. A weekend excursion – even a 'long weekend' – by the normal route was cramped with little time left for the slopes. The answer, albeit an expensive one, Mark had established, was to fly directly with a Swiss regional airline, Air Engiadina, from Zurich to Samedan, a small airport just outside St Moritz, and this is what Mark had arranged for their end-of-season fling. After an early start in London, the thirty-minute flight from Zurich to Samedan meant that, even allowing for the hour's time difference between the UK and Switzerland, they would still be able to get in some afternoon skiing.

At Samedan, they were met by the hotel car which, within ten minutes, was depositing them at the entrance to the Palace in the middle of St Moritz. The Palace was thought by some to be the best hotel in the town, although this was not the opinion of the Swiss, who rarely stayed there. However, there was no disputing the fact that the Palace was the place to be for those who enjoyed an ostentatious display of wealth. Mark Palmer felt quite at home.

Mark and his party quickly changed, collected their skis and ski-boots from the Palace ski-room, and were then taken in the hotel car on the two-minute journey to the funicular railway, which went to the Corviglia ski area. Within an hour of arriving at Samedan, they were skiing under a typical St Moritz-blue sky, and in brilliant sunshine.

One of the pleasures of spring skiing was that the days were much longer. However, the warmer weather meant that after-lunch skiing was often in snow that had taken on the texture and consistency of rice pudding. It could be wet and heavy, and also dangerous. To avoid this, Mark led the way to the higher slopes around Piz Nair, where the temperature was lower and the snow conditions superb. At the end of three glorious hours, they were able to ski the whole way down to the town, despite the wet and now fast-disappearing snow at the lower levels. They returned to the hotel after a perfect, exhilarating start to the weekend. Mark was quick to point out that, had they travelled from Zurich in the conventional manner, they would still be on the train.

Gail and Helen's tentative programme for the next two days had been to go cross-country skiing along the many langlauf trails that crossed the still frozen lakes and snow-covered meadows of the Engadine valley. The state of the deteriorating late-season snow had, however, brought about a change of plan, and they had now arranged two days of walks along the paths through the woods to the neighbouring towns of Celerina and Pontresina. Mark and Paul were to continue downhill skiing with a guide, Rudi.

Rudi, an instructor with the Palace ski-school, was born and had lived all of his life in the nearby village of Champfer. He knew every inch of the mountain ranges that encircled St Moritz, including rarely explored areas that were accessible for only short periods of the year. Mark had skied with Rudi for many years, and they would usually ski together two or three times each season. This Saturday morning they were to ski the more challenging Corvatsch mountain and they planned to spend most of the time off-piste.

By midday both Mark and Paul were hot and weary; Paul because he was not as accomplished a skier as Mark, and Mark because he was overweight and not as fit as he used to be. They stopped for a long, leisurely – and, as it turned out, fairly liquid – lunch at a mountain restaurant at the foot of the chairlift. At a nearby table were three American women. As Mark poured from the third bottle of wine, his always loud voice dominated the restaurant. And, increasingly, his conversation was aimed at entertaining the American table with what he thought were his amusing asides.

After lunch the two groups left the restaurant for the chairlift at about the same time. The lift was not one of the new sleek and fast machines which accommodate six or even eight people, but an old-fashioned two-seater. As Mark reached the lift, the American woman who had particularly attracted his attention – tall, with long, flowing jet-black hair and a vivid yellow ski-suit – was standing alone. Her two companions had just been whisked away and she, in turn, was waiting for the next chair on the lift to arrive. Seeing his opportunity, he was at her side in a flash just as the chair appeared; and, before she had a moment to exclaim, they were lifted away sitting together side by side.

It was a long slow ride and Mark had ample time to get to know his new acquaintance. Her name was Jane and she came from New York. She was a lawyer working for a bank in Manhattan and had recently been divorced. 'My two friends, Susan and Estelle, have been coming here for years,' she volunteered. 'They are both older,' she said archly, 'but,' now giggling, 'their husbands are *really* old.' Recovering herself, she continued, more sedately, 'They come to St Moritz every January. The husbands don't ski, but they are keen on a strange sport called curling. Do you know anything about it?'

'A little,' Mark replied, 'there are several rinks by the Carlton in St Moritz and I've watched them curling there. It's like crown green bowls on ice. I think that it originated in Scotland. And it *is* a strange game. It has a language all of its own.

'It's all supervised by a "skip", who seems, at least at the Carlton, to spend most of his time swearing at his team in Swiss-German. A "stone" is delivered – "lay" they call it – towards a "dolly", which sits in the middle of what they call a "house", and the person who gets his stone closest to the dolly is the winner. Something like that. The most extraordinary sight, though, is that of the other members of the team – the "sweepers" – brushing the ice with their brooms like dervishes as they try to encourage the stone into the house, while at the same time chanting "ja", "ja", "ja".'

'Well, we are staying at the Suvretta House and it has its own rink although nobody seems to be using it at the moment,' she said, now looking towards him with a dazzling smile on her very full lips.

'I guess the conditions aren't right,' Mark responded. 'It's far too warm. The stone would probably fall right through the ice.'

The Suvretta House was a large five-star hotel on the edge of St Moritz, with its own direct access to the ski-slopes. It was in a more traditional and understated style than the Palace, and Mark had visited it only infrequently.

'Susan and Estelle are here for spring skiing, this time without their husbands, and they persuaded me to join them because I was feeling low after the divorce,' Jane said, changing subjects. 'It's my first time skiing in Europe, and I think it's great. Usually I go to Colorado and sometimes to Vermont. But Vermont has so much ice and stuff; and it's so cold! I prefer it here,' she said, favouring him with another of her now regular, warm, wide-mouthed smiles. At which point they reached the top of the lift. They were now on very friendly terms, but she had to rejoin Susan and Estelle while Mark waited for Paul and Rudi, who were in the chair immediately behind.

Throughout the rest of the afternoon, Mark's pulse raced as he caught an occasional glimpse of the distinctive yellow ski-suit. He had established where she and her two friends were lunching the next day.

After dinner in the grill room of the Palace, Mark and Gail, and Paul and Helen repaired to the hotel's bar, where Mark's braying, boastful voice soon attracted attention. A large man, who had been drinking alone at the bar, introduced himself. 'Hello,' he said, 'Michael Fisher,' with a slight bow. 'You seem to be having a good time, and you are obviously from England. Whereabouts?'

'London,' said Mark.

'Well, so am I,' said the new arrival.

'Gail, Paul, Helen,' said Mark as he went round the table, 'and I'm Mark. Come and join us.'

Michael Fisher sat down at their table and was soon an animated member of the group. He really was a very large man indeed. His weight must have been more than twenty stone and, although he was certainly over six feet in height, his overall bulk meant that he did not look tall. He had small, round, piggy eyes buried within a heavy fleshy face. His hair had disappeared entirely from the top of his head, and all that remained were a number of long silky strands at the sides and some furry patches at the back. Despite his unprepossessing appearance, he was a lively conversationalist. At first glance

21

one might have thought that he was about 50 years of age but, on closer scrutiny, it became clear that he was much younger. As he entertained them with a story about his approach to life, it turned out that he had, in fact, recently had his 35th birthday.

'Both my father and my grandfather died in their forties from heart problems. I believe, very strongly, that these things are hereditary; that longevity, or in my case the lack of it, is determined by family history, that it is in the genes. So, I do not expect to live beyond my fiftieth year,' he said in a matter-of-fact manner. 'The result is,' Michael continued, 'that I live my life on the assumption that I have no more than fifteen years left. I live each day to the full. I work hard, and I play hard.'

Even Mark felt inhibited from making the obvious point that that particular lifestyle and its visible effects on his weight and health might involve a certain amount of subconscious wish-fulfilment. But what really caught Mark's imagination was Michael's work. He was a venture capitalist, and it was from the ample rewards of his business activities that he financed his several-week stays at the Palace. Mark encouraged Michael to describe the kinds of businesses in which he invested, but was careful not to pitch his questions too closely to his own business affairs as he did not want to alert Paul to the problems of Palmer Industries. What he did say to Michael was that it would be interesting to talk again, in London, and business cards were exchanged.

It was at this point that Michael announced his intention to go down to the King's Club, and he pressed Mark and his party to join him. The King's Club was a nightclub situated within the Palace, where the fashionable rich of St Moritz gathered together sometime after midnight. Members of the Agnelli, Niarchos and Onassis dynasties were among the many of Europe's super-rich families who owned chalets in St Moritz and the King's Club was not short of the right kind of custom. However, Gail knew from a previous visit that, in addition to wealthy jet-setters, there were also usually a number of scantily clad ladies of uncertain background sitting at the bar, and she was unwilling to allow Mark's ever-eager eyes to enjoy that particular feast. She said that they had had a long day, had an early start the following morning, and insisted that she and Mark must now go to their room.

On Sunday morning Mark's first thoughts were of Jane. He told Paul and Rudi that they should all ski on the Corviglia side of St Moritz – where they had spent the Friday afternoon – as he wanted to be within easy reach of the restaurant where he knew that Jane was to have lunch. Mark was restless and preoccupied during the course of the morning and he rarely joined in the banter and badinage that were the normal background to the sheer exhilaration of skiing high in the mountains under a clear blue sky. Paul and Rudi were left very much to their own devices. Soon after twelve o'clock, Mark was pushing the party in the direction of the Chaselas mountain restaurant. Chaselas was a smart and popular place for lunch, situated at the base of the Suvretta mountain, just above the Suvretta House. They reached the restaurant before the Americans and Mark smoothly organised a table next to the one reserved by Jane and her friends. When Jane arrived, Mark thought that she seemed as pleased to see him as he was to see her and by the time the wine had appeared the two tables had been moved together to become one.

Lunch proceeded in a party atmosphere but Mark was momentarily disconcerted when he heard that the three women had stopped skiing for the day and were to return to the hotel after lunch. Susan and Estelle had arranged for a massage at what was described as the 'Suvretta Wellness Centre', and Jane had planned to go down with them. However, she was easily persuaded that there was no need for her to finish so early, and she happily agreed to spend the afternoon skiing with Mark, Paul and Rudi. As Susan and Estelle commented, they could at least take comfort, while deserting her, from the fact that there was safety in numbers.

The pattern of the afternoon's skiing was set when Mark and Jane raced off together on the first run, some way ahead of Paul and Rudi. They skied together, rode the lifts together and seemed largely oblivious of their other, supposed, companions. They would ride chairlifts, which could comfortably have accommodated four people, but they would arrive breathlessly at the lift ahead of the others and quickly jump on the chair and pull down the barrier before Paul and Rudi had arrived. And these new chairlifts, with their all-embracing wind covers, provided a certain amount of privacy.

Rudi's working day normally finished at four o'clock and it was usual for them to ski back to the hotel at about that time. When the time arrived, however, Mark did not want to stop. 'I want to do just one more run,' he said.

Paul was not happy. 'But Mark, you know that we've arranged to take Gail and Helen to Hanselmann's at five o'clock and even one more run will make us late,' he said.

Mark persisted. He said to Paul, 'You ski down with Rudi, meet Gail and Helen, take them to Hanselmann's, and explain to them that I will join them there. We will most likely all arrive at the tea house at about the same time anyway.' Paul was more than sceptical, but as usual, Mark had his way.

Mark and Jane pushed off, in a fever of intoxication at the fact that they were at last alone together, to start what they had promised would be the last run of the day. They paused, halfway down the mountain, to catch their breath, and to take in again the spellbinding scenery; the mountains which one felt one could almost touch and, below, the valley and lakes of the Engadine which stretched into the far distance. It was all so beautiful they did not want the spell to be broken, and for it all to come to an end. They agreed that they should stop for a final, and very quick, glass of champagne at the small hut where they served drinks and sandwiches, at the bottom of the ski-lift.

As they sipped their champagne, sitting on a bench in a corner of the mountain hut, they could hardly keep their hands off each other. Jane felt an extraordinary sense of freedom and excitement. She could hardly remember ever having enjoyed such a good time. She had not realised until now how stressful the divorce must have been, and how it had affected her. But here, in a foreign country, and in the mountains with the snow and the sun – and now the champagne – she felt an entirely new – and free – woman. And she felt so happy being with Mark. He was so different from the stereotypical, buttoned-down, conservative Englishmen she had occasionally met in her

24

work at the bank. And he was a dream of a skier. She, herself, had rarely skied better as she followed him down the mountains – never more than a dozen feet behind – trying to reproduce, but not quite matching, his accomplished and aggressive style as he attacked the slopes (his years of expensive early lessons had paid off).

She had displayed a boldness and an abandon which was quite different from what she thought to be her usual character. And Mark was not slow to take advantage of this. He was always ready for a fling with a new and attractive woman. He reminded her that he was returning to London the following day. And then he said that he had an idea. 'The lavatories are at the bottom of a flight of stairs at the opposite end of the hut. There is,' he whispered, 'a single entrance for men and women, and both share the same washbasins. But,' he said with added emphasis, 'on either side of the washbasins are separate closed cubicles, one side for men and the other side for women.'

As Jane realised what Mark was proposing, she rose from the bench, walked slowly across the room and went down the stairs. Half a minute later, Mark followed. As he came through the door to the lavatories, he saw Jane rather self-consciously washing her hands at one of the washbasins; another woman was similarly engaged at a second washbasin. Mark passed them both, and tested the door of the first of the men's cubicles to confirm that it was free. He went in and pushed the door to while listening intently. As soon as he heard the sound of departing footsteps, he opened the door to pull in a very willing Jane.

As he locked the door behind them, he put his fingers to his lips. There were new sounds of movement outside. Then, as of one mind, their fumbling fingers plucked feverishly at their fastenings as they wordlessly began to battle with the impracticalities of the all-in-one ski-suit. When they were finally able to hold each other, clutching closely, their inhibitions fell away, and the noises could hardly be disguised. But by then they were past caring.

As Jane looked at the ski-suits and the variety of undergarments gathered around their ski-boots, she could hardly repress a giggle at the incongruity of it all. But Mark quickly put his finger, this time to her lips, as he remembered, belatedly, exactly where they were.

25

They hurriedly re-dressed. When they retraced their steps up the stairs, the hut was deserted apart from two waiters who were clearing away the glasses and placing the chairs upside down on the tables. They quickly went to their skis, which were standing alone in the rack; everybody seemed to have left. They walked with their skis the few steps to the ski-lift but, to their horror, saw that the lift was no longer operating. There was only one person to be seen, and he was casually shovelling snow to cover some bare patches by the lift. He made it clear that the lift was closed for the day and could not be re-opened. Yet, without the lift, it was impossible for them to get home to their hotels.

Through a mixture of German, Italian and English, and a liberal array of gestures, they tried to explain their predicament to him. Eventually a compromise was struck. He agreed to start the lift and said that they could then travel on it until they reached the crest of the next slope when they must jump off. From there, he said, they could ski down to the Suvretta House. The lift was one of the few remaining old-fashioned drags lifts, in the form of a T-bar, and it was for security reasons, he said, that he could not allow them to stay on the lift once they were out of his vision. He was already breaking regulations, he explained, as all the other workmen had left for home, and he was not allowed to operate the lift alone. They had no alternative but to go along with his suggestion; but it meant that Mark was going to be horrendously late. He had planned to ski across to Corviglia from the top of the ski-lift and then down to the town. Now, he would have to go with Jane to the Suvretta House and then get a taxi from there to the Palace. He was going to have a lot of explaining to do.

When Mark arrived at the Palace, it was almost seven o'clock. He went straight to their room, where Gail was waiting for him. 'Where have *you* been?' she said, before he could utter a word. 'We waited for you for more than an hour at Hanselmann's.'

'The lifts stopped, I had to ski down to the Suvretta House and then get a taxi,'he replied, his voice fading. She looked at him with stony, disbelieving eyes as he sought to avoid her gaze.

The situation was not a new one for Mark. His infidelities had been the cause of both divorces. Nevertheless, he realised the scale of the betrayal that was involved and something of the pain that Gail must feel. Gail was cold and unforgiving, not that Mark had asked for forgiveness or even suggested that there was anything to forgive. She had her strong suspicions but she could not be certain. Direct confrontation would involve too many risks. But in her heart of hearts she really knew; she had known of his reputation before they were married and events since then had only served to confirm it.

The skiing party on Monday morning was back to the original four. But Mark's thoughts were still with Jane, and the sparkle of the previous two days was missing. The weather had also changed, and the clear skies and crystal-sharp visibility had given way to cloud, a soft, southerly wind – the Föhn – which is inimical to good skiing conditions, and the accompanying 'flat' light, which is one of the less attractive features of skiing in the Alps. The ski-pistes were mainly above the tree line and, without sun, the lack of any contrast made it difficult to determine contours; a single whiteness stretched to the horizon, and seemed to merge with the sky. When skiing, it was not possible to tell whether the piste was rising or falling and Gail, in particular, found that the conditions made her feel disoriented and nauseous. The familiar symptoms were similar to those from travel sickness. Gail soon pleaded that she had had enough, and they stopped for an early lunch at Chesa Veglia, in the centre of the town.

In the afternoon, they went for a desultory stroll around the expensive boutiques that surrounded the Palace before preparing for the journey home. Mark had been able to make a furtive telephone call to Jane from the hotel lobby, and he was to speak to her again from London. She was staying at the Suvretta until the end of the week.

However, thoughts of London brought about the realisation that the return home would mean that he must again confront his financial problems. He had determined that he would talk to Jeremy about venture capital. Michael Fisher's investment funds seemed to have pots of money. They were to catch the plane from Samedan at five o'clock.

CHAPTER FOUR

Gerald Howard had been chairman of Tudor Holdings plc for twelve years. After university, redbrick, he had qualified as an accountant with one of the large City firms. He had then spent five years in the corporate finance department of a middle-ranking merchant bank, where he had achieved some success in advising the bank's clients on take overs. The bank had also had an investment department, and one of its less successful investments had been represented by a large shareholding in a small public company which had fallen upon hard times. The company was Tudor Plastics Ltd, a manufacturer of plastic extrusions.

Gerald, at the age of 32, was given his big opportunity when the bank used its voting power to parachute him into Tudor as its new chairman and chief executive. Gerald was not quite sure what a plastic extrusion was, but this had not been thought to be important as the plan was to build Tudor into a widely diversified conglomerate in tune with the then current stock-market fashion. It was to become a 'hot' stock. He had more than justified the confidence that had been placed in him at such an early age. Tudor Holdings plc, as it was renamed, had been one of the top performing shares of the past decade. This had been brought about by a non-stop series of acquisitions, usually in unrelated fields, financed by the issue of more and more shares at higher and higher prices. It was not certain that the underlying trading performance of the companies acquired had improved under Tudor's management, or that the acquisitions had been made on terms which were particularly favourable to the buyer. But Gerald had succeeded by giving the stock market exactly what it wanted. He accepted totally the City culture of 'no surprises'. If shareholders wanted a smooth, consistent and predictable annual growth in earnings per share, then that was what they would get. Gerald had used to the full the opportunities open to him to improve profits by acquisition accounting and other profit-enhancing accounting techniques – not real profits, of course, but nobody had cared, so long as the figures added up, met expectations, and kept the stock market happy. And keeping the stock market happy (which included his shareholders, not least the largest – the influential Rainbow Asset Management) was what Gerald Howard was all about.

He had received the *Guardian* Young Businessman of the Year award; an honour that had often been the kiss-of-death to its previous recipients. But, so far, Gerald had been spared the perils of the curse of the *Guardian*. When the Cadbury Report on corporate governance was published, he had been one of the first to bring his company fully into line with its proposals. He had separated the roles of chairman and chief executive, appointing one of his colleagues as chief executive, and confining his own position to that of executive chairman. He had also appointed, as recommended, a remuneration committee to fix directors' salaries and benefits. All of this had pleased the City, but it was no more than cosmetics. Gerald had still exercised total autocratic rule at Tudor and the non-executive directors on the remuneration committee had merely sanctified the generous package of benefits which Gerald received from the company, and which had continued to grow, but now at slightly more than the rate that had applied previously.

Gerald was now 44. He was about six feet tall, with a slim, athletic build, and a pale, sharp-featured face. His dull black hair was a little long at the sides and the back, and was cut in a style which might have been fashionable ten years ago. The overall effect was slightly sinister and threatening. He was keen on competitive sport and, as in business, hated losing. He had many admirers, but few friends. His working day was very much head-office bound. He rarely left his Knightsbridge desk. He did not visit other people, they came to him. Although Tudor now had subsidiaries in many parts of the country, and also had a number of overseas operations, they were only rarely visited by Gerald. He had no interest in factories, or products, and even less interest in people. What the operating companies actually did was of no concern to him; his only thought or care was for their perform-ance, represented by the profit figure on the bottom line.

Gerald's finance director, Anthony Kemp, had been with Tudor for five years. He was in his late thirties, was small in stature, and had strong black hair which ran without interruption into a vigorous beard. He had been cruelly but accurately described by an unfriendly stockbroker's analyst as 'looking like a rat with its head pushed through a lavatory brush'. He had an anxious-to-please manner, and an over-zealous approach to his work. He shared with his chairman a single-minded obsession with profit. And, while Gerald's main objective in life was to please the stock market, Anthony's overriding priority was to please Gerald.

Gerald was now in a meeting with his finance director in his Knightsbridge office. They had been closeted together for more than two hours. They were reviewing the latest forecast of profits which had been prepared by the finance director's staff.

Each month a revised forecast was made of profit expectations for the year as a whole to accompany the management accounts. Usually there would be little change from the previous month's forecast, although, most often, there would be an improvement because the accountants in the finance department were only too well aware – he told them so often enough – that Gerald Howard only liked to see good figures. However, for the third successive month, the forecast they were now looking at showed a reduction. And there was little time left in the current accounting year, which ran to the end of September, for this trend to be reversed.

They had looked together at every possible way in which the situation might be improved. It was already too late for any action to be taken by the subsidiaries which might help the underlying trading performance – such as cost reductions or new sales initiatives. There was just not enough time left for any material impact to be felt before the year end.

They had spent most of the meeting discussing cosmetic changes that could improve the way in which the figures were presented or perceived. But even Anthony Kemp's fertile imagination could conjure up no new profits-flattering technique. They had all been exhausted in previous years. And the City would not wear any further changes in accounting policies. The company pension fund had already been raided to add to the year's profits. When this had first been contemplated, Gerald had asked how the auditors could be satisfied that the pension fund would still meet the statutory funding requirement. Anthony had said that it should not present a problem as the actuaries were always very co-operative and would simply alter the assumptions that they had used for future inflation, incomes growth and rates of investment return. There was the slight risk of a sudden fall in the stock market, he had said but, he had argued, even if that should happen there would still be plenty of time for things to improve before the bulk of the pension obligations would need to be met. Gerald had been only too anxious to allow himself to be convinced. But still, it had not been enough. Gerald was beginning to feel unwell. The figures they were looking at would mean that they would not be able to meet the profit expectations of the City. And, if they were certain that this was really the case, they had an obligation to inform the Stock Exchange. A profits warning. Never, in his so far unblemished and mercurial career, had he ever even contemplated such a prospect.

However, Gerald had recognised that there was one last chance. An acquisition. It was still just about possible to complete a takeover in time for it to make a crucial contribution to the year's profits. But they must act quickly. First, they had to identify a candidate. Anthony was given the task of placing a call to Gresham's, their merchant bank. The senior directors of merchant banks do not often leave their offices to meet clients; the clients go to the bank. But Gerald Howard's idiosyncrasies were widely known, and there was no difficulty in arranging a meeting, at Tudor's offices, for the following day.

Gresham's Bank had an aristocratic background and impeccable connections. It had retained its independence when most of its peers had been absorbed by the new breed of sprawling, faceless, multi-national banks. Many of the oldest and best known banks in the City were now owned by foreign banks – Dutch, French, German, American – anything it seemed but British. And the names of these banks, which had taken several generations to establish and for which a 'premium' price had usually been paid, had been replaced almost overnight by a series of meaningless and anonymous initials – ABC Banking Corporation could have been one of them – amid a clash of cultures and mutual incomprehension.

But there had been a price to pay for Gresham's continuing independence. It had built its reputation on being very choosy about its clients. Its relationship with many of those who had been privileged to become clients stretched back into the nineteenth century. In its early days, it had acted for a number of the crowned heads of Europe. It still retained close links with the wealthy and landed aristocracy – and some of the younger family members were to be found in its boardroom. However, the more competitive marketplace, which had been created by the 'big bang' City reforms and by the subsequent arrival of the overseas banks, had meant that new strains had been imposed on these traditional relationships. Clients for whom Gresham's had acted for generations were now being pursued by new competitors. Transaction banking rather than relationship banking was now the vogue.

Clients were encouraged to shop around for fresh advisers for each new transaction – an acquisition, a disposal, or a fund-raising exercise – rather than simply continuing with their traditional, long-time merchant banker. The reward for the client would be lower transaction costs; but the risk, which could not of course be quanti-fied in the same way, was an adviser who would not be as familiar with his client's business and who might not therefore act in his client's best interest.

Gresham's Bank's decision that it was to continue as an independent bank – a decision reached after much heart-searching – had meant that it had needed to respond to these new competitive pressures. Part of the response had been a willingness to consider new clients from a broader spectrum. Clients who had not been from quite the same top drawer, and who were a little short on history.

Nothing quite so vulgar as actually going out and pitching for business – but a new preparedness to react more positively to new introductions. And of course the word had soon got about. Which was how Tudor Holdings had come to be introduced to, and then became a client of, Gresham's Bank.

Although Gresham's had had to bend to the winds of this new competitive environment, it did not feel comfortable within it. And some of its directors felt distinctly queasy in their dealings with a number of their new – and what they saw as upstart – clients.

Gerald's meeting with Gresham's did not go well. The Gresham's delegation was led by a senior director, James Gordon, whose career at the bank, after Eton and a spell as a Guards officer, had been one of effortless, well-connected progression. His six-feet-and-four-inches stature and his patrician manner created an imposing and impressive presence and he was rarely flustered. His reputation for unflap-pability, however, was placed under serious risk as the meeting progressed. He was sceptical about the prospects of completing an acquisition within the tight time scale which Gerald had indicated. He questioned the need for such urgency. Gerald, of course, had to tread carefully. He had not wanted to alarm the bankers about Tudor's trading prospects. That would have alerted them to the possible need for a formal statement to the Stock Exchange – the dreaded profits warning. At the same time, he had to impress upon them the need to act quickly.

Towards the end of the meeting, Gerald lost his temper. 'I know what I want,' he said, his voice rising. 'I believe that an acquisition now is important to maintain the momentum of Tudor's growth. You should go away and do as I ask. I am the one who pays your fees – and this is a way in which you can submit yet another fat bill.' Because, as he had reminded them, he only paid fees on a success basis. They left the meeting with some of their elegant feathers a little ruffled.

Gordon returned to the bank in a vile mood. He was not used to being shouted at – certainly not from people he considered his social inferiors – and he had not enjoyed the experience. He was now closeted with colleagues to consider the next move. Despite their reservations, they knew that they could not afford to be too fastidious and that they had little alternative but to start the trawl of finding a suitable acquisition candidate for Tudor. This was where the strength of their fabled connections and networking skills would be put to the test.

CHAPTER FIVE

'It is just a blip,' said Sarah, in response to questions about the recent investment performance, 'and I am not going to be pushed into changing a policy which has been so successful.'

It was the beginning of March, and Sarah Armstrong was chairing her regular morning conference, as head of Rainbow Asset Management, known throughout the City by its acronym, RAM, and by some of the less deferential members of the financial community as RAMBO. She was one of the City's new 'stars', having been poached from a rival fund management group three years ago and, like some Premier League footballer, having received a 'signing-on' fee of £1 million. She was the David Beckham of the City.

It was only recently that fund management had come to be regarded as at all glamorous. The bids and deals of corporate finance had traditionally been thought to be the sexiest area of banking; and it was corporate finance that had attracted the heavy-hitters, and that had offered the highest rewards. But now the pecking order had been reversed. Fund managers, who had previously been unknown and unsung backroom boys (and girls) were now high-profile, front-line stormtroopers. And while the macho world of corporate finance had been dominated by men, in money management it was more often the women who were on top.

Sarah had been fortunate to have started her career at the time the exponential growth of funds under management was bringing about this change. At more than £500 billion, these funds now dominated the stock market, accounting for 80 per cent of total investment.

Pension funds, with their historically benign tax regime, had been the powerhouse behind this growth. But the market was not just large, it was also very profitable. The managers took a percentage of the funds which were under their control and, unlike corporate finance where the profits depended upon volatile take-over activity, the profits from money management were predictable and grew steadily each year. The stock market placed a high value on such quality earnings and this had made the shareholders of the management companies extremely rich.

The funds under Sarah's control accounted for a large slice of this lucrative market. She was a powerful lady. The media had made a cult figure of Sarah, and this was something that she had not discouraged. The interest extended far beyond the financial press to glossy magazines, which had produced lengthy features inter-spersed with glamorous photographs, and even to the tabloids. Of course, she had complained about the trivialisation of issues, and of the sexist nature of much that was written. When she read the inevitable references to the different outfits and their expensive designer labels that she wore for work, a different one for each day – Sarah as a clothes horse – she would exclaim disdainfully that there were successful men working in the City who changed their Savile Row suits each day and that went by without comment. But her obvious and wholehearted co-operation with her alleged exploiters meant that her complaints carried little weight.

Sarah justified her easy accessibility to the press by claiming that it was simply part of the overall marketing effort and that the high profile helped RAM to obtain new business. It had certainly done no harm to Sarah's career.

The media interest could not have been sustained, however, without Sarah's extraordinary success in managing the assets under her control. Her funds had been top of the investment performance tables in each of the two completed years since she had jumped ship. This had been brought about by an aggressive investment policy which involved a typical RAM portfolio holding shares in no more than 40 to 50 separate companies rather than the more conventional 200 to 300, with as much as five to eight per cent of a portfolio invested in just one stock. This lack of spread and balance increased risk but, if the stock selection was right, the rewards and the relative out-performance could be significant. And this had proved to be the case with Sarah's funds.

The long bull-market run had been a critical factor in the success of this policy, particularly as much of the stock market growth had been fuelled by the rapidly rising share prices of the newly fashionable high technology companies in which RAM had invested. Another feature of what had become a virtuous circle was that the sheer size of RAM's funds and their concentration on a relatively small number of companies meant that it was usually the largest shareholder on the register. And the identification with such a prestigious shareholder as RAM improved the stock market rating of the company in which shares were held.

RAM was also influential in improving the share prices of its investments in other ways. It established a close relationship with each of these favoured companies and was privy to their strategy. It could be influential in resolving takeover battles. If RAM held shares in both of the companies involved in a takeover, and Sarah believed that two plus two might well equal more than four – at least in respect of the short-term performance of their respective share prices – she would not be shy at delivering its shareholding in the target company into the eager and then everlastingly grateful hands of the bidder. For example, RAM, as the largest shareholder in Tudor Holdings, had been helpful in smoothing the way forward for its apparently effortless progression.

Sarah enjoyed her power. She was ruthless in her pursuit of success and felt no loyalty to the company in which she was invested. If a company's results did not live up to her expectations, or if its executives disappointed her in some other way, she would have no compunction about ditching her shareholding. And the first time the stock market would hear the news would be with the publication of the formal announcement that RAM had sold its stake; which could have devastating consequences for the share price of the abandoned company, and severe implications for the future career prospects of its slighted executives. And where the shareholding in an offending company was too large to be disposed of in an orderly manner, Sarah had been known to lean heavily on the non-executive directors of the company concerned to bring about a change in its management.

Sarah's success meant that she was not only powerful, but also wealthy. In addition to the £1 million 'golden hello' which she had received when joining RAM, a combination of her salary and a generous performance-related bonus meant that she earned more than £1 million each year. But this was not all. She had options on shares in RAM which were exercisable in two years' time (five years after her arrival), and which had a current market value in excess of £20 million. The star of the City, therefore, was even more highly rewarded than the stars of soccer, as even David Beckham had not been given shares in Manchester United. And her total remuneration package dwarfed that of many of the so-called fat cats who ran the companies in which she had invested, and who actually produced things, rather than simply dealing with money.

Sarah was thought to be still in her thirties – just – although her date of birth was not shown in *Who's Who*, in which she had appeared for the first time in its most recent edition. She lived in a Holland Park mansion (which she had bought two years ago for £2 million and which was now said to be worth around £5 million) with her long-term partner, Simon, and their two children, twin girls. Simon was not quite a 'house husband' as the Holland Park establishment boasted a full-time, live-in housekeeper and a nanny, who had been retained despite the fact that the twins were now spending most of their days at school, where they had recently started. However, he had not had a 'proper job' since he was culled five years ago (just after the birth of the twins) in one of the periodic bouts of redundancies in which the City's stockbroking houses seem to indulge as business ebbs and flows. He had been employed as an analyst in the oil sector and it had suited both Simon and Sarah for him not to seek another full-time job, but to work on a part-time basis from home on a number of consultancy projects, while helping Sarah to balance her high-powered working life with the demands of looking after the twins and their home. It seemed to have worked.

Sarah's desk was situated at the apex of an open-plan office from which she could survey her team of fund managers. Each manager was in charge of a number of specific portfolios, and the high degree of personal responsibility and discretion which they each enjoyed was one of the other defining characteristics of the RAM approach to fund management.

There were a number of internal procedures that were meant to control risk within certain parameters, but these were much less tightly drawn than those of RAM's competitors. Formalities were kept to a minimum. Flair and individuality in stock selection, which was crucial given the small number of shares in which the funds were invested, were encouraged. RAM did not run with the herd. It was not quite backing hunches but sometimes it was not far short of that.

Observers detected a gung-ho attitude and a feeling of invincibility, which many found unpalatable. RAM's executives, as exemplified by Sarah, gave the impression that they were the new Masters – and Mistresses – of the Universe. Sarah's public persona was of a forbidding presence. She wore expensive, severely tailored suits of impeccable taste – the media were not wrong in highlighting her interest in clothes. She had a firm upright posture, with her head seemingly tilted a little backwards and her long and slightly pointed chin jutting aggressively forwards as if in compensation. This, together with her more than averagely high heels and the fact that her thick, strong, burnished, reddish-brown hair was layered in an almost bouffant style (it was groomed twice weekly at Michaeljohn) made her appear taller than she was. The overall effect was one of arrogance and of a person who would certainly stand out in a crowd but whom one would not seek out for small talk. Behind her contact lenses her eyes were a lapis lazuli blue, and she rarely smiled. It was a mask which never slipped at work, but one which was quickly discarded when among family and friends. There she was warm and loving, and generous with her affections. A totally different person.

Its performance in the first three-quarters of Sarah's third year at the helm had maintained RAM's position at the top of the table. However, the value of funds under management was measured daily, and the pressure to perform, day-in, day-out, quarter after quarter, was relentless. The first weeks of the final quarter of the year had seen some weakening in RAM's relative performance. The Stock Market had faltered, and some of RAM's key investments, which had out-performed the market on the way up, were now showing a bigger decline on the way down. There were suggestions that the long bull-run might be at an end, and that a bear market was in prospect. Although relative performance figures for the final quarter and for the calendar year as a whole had not yet been published, some of RAM's critics thought that they could see the first hint of hairline cracks in its façade. Sarah would hear none of this and, with her mask firmly in place, had been prompted to make her dismissive, throwaway comment: 'It is merely a blip.' It was a phrase that would come back to haunt her.

CHAPTER SIX

When Mark arrived in his office on the Tuesday morning after his return from St Moritz, he immediately telephoned Jane at the Suvretta. It was nine o'clock London time and, therefore, with the hour's time difference, ten o'clock in Switzerland. Jane would normally already have left for the slopes but, as Mark had arranged to call at this time, she was still in her room, waiting, when the call was put through.

As she heard his voice, she blurted out, straightaway, without any preliminaries. 'It's fantastic!' This, Mark quickly learned, was not a reaction to the sound of his voice, but a comment on the weather. 'We had a metre of snow overnight,' Jane said, breathlessly, 'and now the sky's cleared and there's not a cloud to be seen. It's quite, quite incredible.'

'That's absolutely typical,' said Mark. 'Every year it's the same. Just as the resort is about to close, there is a dump of new snow and you have the best conditions of the season.'

'Well, I'm here for the rest of the week,' said Jane, 'and I'm going to make the most of it.'

Mark was put out by this. He had hoped for a different reason for her excitement. 'Look, I've had an idea. You told me that you are staying at the Suvretta until Sunday, when the hotel closes, and I think you said that you were then to stay in Zurich overnight so that you could catch an early flight back to New York on the Monday morning.'

'That's right.'

41

'Well, why not come to London on the Sunday, stay in a hotel near the airport where I can join you, and then fly back to New York from Heathrow? There's bound to be room on an early flight on the following morning.'

Jane was immediately interested. 'That's a wonderful idea. That really would be great.' There was a brief interruption as Jane was called away from the telephone. 'Darling,' she said, as she came back on the line, 'I must go now because I'm keeping people waiting. But I will speak to the concierge, see if he can make the arrangements and call you again this evening, six o'clock your time. Ciao.' She said briskly, and then she was gone.

Mark replaced the telephone but had no real enthusiasm for dealing with the routine calls and correspondence which had built up while he had been away. He was impatient for six o'clock and the expected call from Jane. And he was downcast at the thought of the snow, and the sun, and the mountains – not to mention lunch and Jane – that he was missing. But then, still dwelling on St Moritz, he remembered Michael Fisher. That cheered him up a little, and he rang Michael's office to make an appointment to see him when he was back in London. The meeting was arranged for the following Monday morning.

He next phoned Jeremy Stephens, told him about the venture capitalist, and asked him to come along. Jeremy was guarded in his response, asked one or two questions, but agreed to join Mark for the Monday meeting. He also told Mark that a date had been fixed to see Chiswells, the merchant bank, for the following week, on the Wednesday, two days after the Michael Fisher meeting. Mark then sat alone, brooding, at his desk. He never really enjoyed his conversations with Jeremy. He could somehow detect the disapproval that he thought lay behind his voice. And he now had no particular appetite for meetings with merchant banks. But it had been his idea. He had to do something to resolve his financial problems, and he did not seem to have any alternatives.

He looked at his watch. It was ten o'clock – eleven o'clock in Switzerland. He could imagine Jane having a marvellous time on the slopes, perhaps now looking forward to lunch – which they would probably enjoy sitting outside, on a terrace, in the sun. When he spoke to her at six, he would make sure that there were no problems in getting her into London at the weekend.

Late on the following Sunday afternoon, Mark was driving his Porsche along the M3 from his weekend Hampshire farmhouse towards Heathrow Airport. He had told Gail that he had an early meeting the following morning with Michael Fisher, which was true, and that to avoid the mad Monday morning congestion on the roads into London he would spend the Sunday night in St John's Wood, which was not true.

Jane had made the promised six o'clock telephone call on the Tuesday (they had also spoken at that time on each subsequent day) and, with a new breathlessness, had told Mark that the concierge had made all the necessary arrangements, that she would be arriving at Heathrow on the Sunday afternoon, and that a room had been booked at a hotel close to the airport.

As Mark left the M3 and joined the M25 before the final few miles to the turn-off for the hotel, he calculated that, with the hour time advantage, Jane should already be settled in their room. He left his car in the hotel car park and, carrying only his briefcase in which he had surreptitiously packed the minimum of overnight requirements, he announced himself at the reception desk. He was told that his 'wife', as the receptionist referred to Jane with practised diplomacy, had already booked in. Mark took the lift to the third floor, located the room and tapped softly on the door. Within seconds, Jane appeared in the doorway, dressed only in a towelling hotel dressing gown. She had obviously just left the shower, and with a squeal of delight she was in his arms. While they embraced and exchanged hungry kisses, she was moving slowly backwards towards the bathroom, clutching him tightly to her body. At the same time Mark was trying to disengage himself of his jacket and trousers in what seemed to be almost a repeat of the St Moritz experience. Soon they were entwined on the still-damp mat on the floor of the bathroom in an explosion of pent-up passion.

*

Mark and Jane had dinner in the hotel dining room. It was in the cold impersonal style typical the world over of the dining facilities provided by hotels catering for itinerant travellers. Only half the tables were occupied. Some of their fellow diners seemed to be passing time as they waited for an onward flight, while others were more obviously nefariously engaged in the same illicit conjunctions as Mark and Jane.

Mark had showered after the bathroom-floor exertions and, lacking any alternative, had re-dressed in the clothes in which he had arrived. As they now talked over dinner, they both realised how little they still knew of each other. Mark was cautious when discussing his domestic arrangements and business life, but Jane was much more open – a reflection of her American background and newly free personal status. Mark was more at ease when talking about St Moritz and when hearing from Jane of the last few days of fabulous skiing. But they were not there to engage in small talk and their thoughts soon returned to the real purpose of their liaison. Without dessert or coffee, they returned to their room; and to their first night together.

At seven o'clock the following day Mark was on the M4 on his way into London in the midst of the already heavy, early Monday morning traffic which Gail had thought he had sought to avoid. He had dropped Jane off at Heathrow's Terminal 3 to catch her New York flight at what, for Mark, was the unearthly hour of six o'clock. There had been a final embrace before the porter trundled away with her baggage, but they had both been too exhausted to exchange more than a few brief, but happy, final words. Mark was to telephone her the next day at her office.

His involvement with Jane had started out as nothing more than an opportunistic holiday fling. But it seemed to be developing into something more than that. Almost an obsession. He could hardly get her out of his mind. And he didn't particularly want to.

Inevitably, he was still wearing the clothes in which he had left home, although he had, at least, secreted a change of underpants in his briefcase. He had shared Jane's toothbrush and he planned to shave at his office. Although he had showered before leaving the hotel, his senses were still alive to the taste and scent of Jane, and his skin still felt her touch on every part of his body. He was hardly of a mind or a mood for work, and yet this was a week in which important decisions might have to be taken which would affect the future of his business. Just before eight o'clock he reached Regent's Park, parked the Porsche in his basement car space and took the lift to his second-floor office.

CHAPTER SEVEN

Jeremy arrived by taxi at nine o'clock and he and a visibly weary Mark walked together the short distance to Portland Place, where Michael Fisher had his office. When Mark had told Jeremy of his discussion with Michael and had said that he thought that an investment by a venture capitalist in Palmer Industries might be the solution to its problems, Jeremy had been deeply sceptical. He knew from his own experience with other clients that the popular perception of a venture capitalist as being some kind of fairy god-mother who makes long-term investments in new businesses was a fallacy. The last thing that today's venture capital fund managers wanted was to be locked in for the longer term; and the word commitment would not even feature in their vocabulary. Jeremy was also aware that, in the unlikely event of Palmer Industries even being considered as suitable for venture capital investment, there would be the same concerns about the calibre of the management and the flawed profit record as there would be for a flotation. Jeremy realised, however, that his negative views had not gone down well with Mark, and he had agreed to join him for the meeting and to keep an open mind.

As they now walked, on a bright spring morning, along the southern edge of Regent's Park and, at Park Crescent, crossed Marylebone Road into Portland Place, Jeremy made a half-hearted attempt at a joke. 'Mark, do you know how you can always recognise a venture capitalist when he walks into a room?'

'No, tell me.'

'The first thing he looks for is the exit.'

This was not well received but Jeremy compounded the problem by adding that from what Mark had said about Michael Fisher's life expectancy, he would be even more concerned than usual to get his money back quickly. Humour was clearly not Jeremy's strong point and in trying to lighten the situation he had only succeeded in making matters worse. Mark was not amused, and he reminded Jeremy of his promise to keep an open mind.

Having heard Mark's description of him, Jeremy was intrigued to meet Michael Fisher. He immediately warmed to the friendly, outgoing personality and to his obvious *joie de vivre*. Michael took them on a tour of his office to show off the various trophies which celebrated his successful deals. He seemed to take greater pleasure from the disposals than the acquisitions – and the gap between the two was often very short. However, soon after the formal start of the meeting, Jeremy's fears were confirmed. Fisher said that an investor would not feel comfortable as a minority shareholder in a private company such as Palmer Industries without a market for its shares and therefore, without any early prospect of a realisation. He did not quite say, 'without an exit', but they got the message. More generally, Michael indicated that his current policy was to devote the whole of the resources of the funds under his management to investments in management buy-outs, where the returns were more certain and more quickly realised. And that, apart from some gossip about St Moritz, was the end of the meeting.

As they walked back to Regent's Park, a chastened Mark asked Jeremy why it seemed to be possible for venture capitalists to make such large amounts of money from management buy-outs. Jeremy expounded, with some vehemence, on an issue which was close to his heart.

'In a management buy-out, the venture capitalist will provide finance to the existing management of a subsidiary company to enable it to acquire its business from its parent company. The venture capital provider will want a very large slice of the equity for the service. The subsidiary's parent will usually be a large corporation pursuing the new fashion for de-merger and focus. But the negotiations, which will precede the acquisition, will not be between equals. The management of the subsidiary will inevitably have more and better information than the remote head office of the parent company. This inside information can, and will be, used to negotiate a deal on terms attractive to the management.'

Jeremy paused at this point, slightly breathless, as they re-crossed Marylebone Road and carefully negotiated the dog-leg of traffic lights. He then quickly resumed. 'Most often, within only two or three years after the deal has been struck, the newly independent subsidiary will be floated on the stock market on the back of miraculously increased profits, which will suddenly have materialised from the hidden reserves established by the now massively incentivised managers. Giving the venture capital investor his all-important and almost risk-free exit. Taking profits which, it could be argued, more properly belonged to its previous owner. While the easy pickings of management buy-outs are around,' Jeremy concluded, as they entered the park, 'you will not meet any poor venture capitalists; and you will not find their funds available for genuine entrepreneurial activity.'

They had now reached Mark's office, where they parted before Mark could make any considered response. Jeremy then continued towards Baker Street, where he was to catch a cab. They were to meet again in two days' time at Chiswells, the merchant bank from which they were to seek the advice that Mark had requested. Mark climbed the stairs to his office. His body felt sore and weary, and tender. And he was beginning to feel dispirited.

CHAPTER EIGHT

Jeremy arrived early at Chiswells and was promptly ushered into one of the many identical, severe and sparsely furnished rooms that were available for meetings with clients. Merchant banks, whose hallmarks were discretion and confidentiality, did not like their visitors to linger in reception areas and risk the embarrassment that might be involved in crossing the path of another caller.

Although Jeremy sought to maintain a discreet distance from what he thought was the unjustified arrogance of most merchant banks, his carefully modulated speech, precise manner and City suit created the impression that he was perfectly at ease in their environment. But, as Jeremy reflected, while staring at the almost blank walls of the meeting room, it had not always been so.

Jeremy came from Rochdale, a small Lancashire mill town to the north and east of Manchester, which had achieved some fame because of its best-known export, the entertainer Gracie Fields. His parents had met in one of the town's many cotton mills. They had both worked in the same weaving shed, his mother, Jean, at a loom and his father, James (but Jimmy to his many friends in the pub) as an overlooker. Now, more than 50 years later, Jeremy still saw and heard in his dreams the 'knocker-up' man, who would rattle his long stick on his parents' bedroom window to ensure that they were awake in time for the seven o'clock start. They had then walked, in their wooden clogs, from their terrace of two-up and two-down houses, the short journey to the mill, which was at the end of their cobbled street.

Jean died when Jeremy was only nine years old. She had always been a sickly woman and her ill-health had been aggravated by the working conditions in the cotton mill and by the problems of childbirth. She had never fully recovered from the birth of Jeremy's brother, John (the family seemed to like names beginning with the letter 'J') three years earlier. James was called up for army service in 1940, but he had seen little of the war, for much of his time had been spent at home on compassionate leave due to his wife's sickness, and the remainder at a 'cushy' local posting. He was a feckless character, and had for many years been a regular at a number of the Rochdale beer houses.

Theirs was a 'mixed' marriage in so far as James was a Catholic and Jean a Protestant. Jean's strongly Protestant family had disowned her and she had no contact with them after her wedding day. She had converted to the Catholic faith and had entered into the usual undertakings to ensure that any children were to be brought up and educated accordingly. Jeremy was attending the local Catholic church school when his mother died.

James was badly affected by the tragedy of his wife's death, and his already established drinking problem became more acute. He was in no state to look after two small boys and they had quickly been parcelled off to his parents' home in Manchester.

Jeremy's grandparents had moved to Manchester a number of years earlier so that his grandfather could take up work with the City Council. He had become the driver of a horse-drawn Corporation delivery cart, and one of Jeremy's happier schoolboy memories was of the special times when he was allowed to sit by his grandfather's side on the top of the cart as he negotiated the narrow streets of his delivery round.

Jeremy was soon enrolled in his new school, St Anne's, in the Ancoats area of Manchester. At dinner time – in the middle of the day – St Anne's Catholic schoolboys would line up on one side of the local 'cut', a minor tributary of the River Irwell, and chuck stones at the Protestant boys of a rival school, similarly lined up on the other side. The Protestant boys would reciprocate.

The religious divisions were sharply drawn. Catholics rarely had Protestant friends, and vice versa. Streets were ruthlessly segregated. In football, Catholics supported – and played for – Manchester United and Protestants for Manchester City. In employment, jobs would routinely be advertised with the postscript, 'Catholics need not apply', and when the department store C&A opened in Manchester, its riposte was that '*Only* Catholics should apply'. Jeremy's grandmother, who was in many ways a saintly woman, had been known to say, innocently, of the non-Catholic tally man, 'He's a Protestant, but he's not a bad man.'

Jeremy did well at St Anne's, although he was not always the happiest of boys. He was teased mercilessly about his name, which his classmates thought was 'soft' and 'sissy'. The name had been a compromise between his parents, his mother not wanting one of the traditional saints' names which were more usual. Despite the dislocation problems caused by the change in schools, Jeremy won a scholarship to one of Manchester's two Catholic grammar schools.

St Bede's College had a reputation as a seminary, but, as well as preparing many of its pupils for the priesthood, it also provided a good grounding for the more worldly professions. Jeremy resisted the inevitable pressures towards a religious vocation and was one of the academically stronger pupils in his year. He was more than averagely successful in his 'O' level examinations, but, in his sixteenth year, once again there was a major disruption to his life. His grandmother died and, after a family conference, it was decided that his brother would stay with one of the aunts in Manchester so that he could complete his education – he was thirteen and still at St Anne's – while Jeremy was to be looked after by another aunt who lived in London, where it was thought his opportunities would be greater. The two brothers parted and were never again to become close.

Jeremy's Auntie Betty, one of Jeremy's father's three sisters, had left Manchester as a teenager to work in one of London's large hotels. She married a Londoner and they had lived there together since the marriage. They had no children. Although the Mancunian part of the family had been close, Jeremy's contact with his aunt had been infrequent, and had mainly been confined to weddings and funerals – of which there were several.

They lived in Streatham in South London, in a cramped 1930s three-bedroomed house. But the house was not rented. It belonged to them – at least subject to the balance of the mortgage – and it had a garden. It was far better than anything that Jeremy had so far experienced.

Auntie Betty's husband had a clerical job as the cashier in the office of an accountant and he commuted each day to the business premises in Holborn. There was no possibility of Jeremy continuing his education as no money was available and it became imperative for him to find a job as soon as possible.

Jeremy had always had a head for figures. During the periodic bouts of his mother's sickness, before her untimely death, when he must have been no more than eight or nine years of age, he would be asked to undertake the family's weekly grocery shopping from the list which she would prepare. He would fulfil this responsibility in a serious and conscientious manner which belied his years, quickly getting to know the prices of all the essentials and never failing to remember the correct 'divi' number so that the purchases would qualify for the annual dividend from the local Co-op.

When he was in his first year at St Bede's, he would then have been about twelve years old, he had devised a money-making game which he called 'The Score'. It was a simple form of lottery based on the total number of points which Wigan's Rugby League football team would score in its Saturday match. Each week, it would usually be on a Sunday morning, Jeremy would cut out 50 slips of paper and write on them each of the numbers nought to 50 (excluding the number one) – the scores. He would then carefully fold the slips and put them all together in a tin box. The remaining part of Sunday, after Mass, he would traipse round to the homes of his various aunts and uncles, and other neighbours, offering the scores at two pennies each; the winner, the one drawing the number which equated to Wigan's score at the subsequent Saturday game, would receive a prize of five shillings. If he sold all the scores, his takings would be eight shillings and four pence, which would mean a profit of three shillings and four pence. A sizeable weekly sum at that time for a twelve-year-old boy. But, sometimes, he did better than that. Wigan was a prolifically high-scoring team and several times each season they would score in excess of fifty points. On those occasions Jeremy kept the five shillings prize money in addition to his three shillings and four pence.

So, work in an accountant's office seemed to offer as good a start as anything, although Jeremy was not quite sure what an accountant actually did. His uncle arranged for him to meet his employer, Bill Foster, to see if there might be an opening.

Bill Foster was a chartered accountant who had set up in business on his own account soon after qualifying. He had been determined to have his independence and to be answerable to nobody. He was a sole practitioner and he traded under the name of Foster & Co. Bill Foster also originated from Lancashire but hailed from the plusher realms of Lytham St Anne's. He took to Jeremy straightaway. Jeremy worked as an assistant audit clerk for a year, after which Mr Foster (as Jeremy was to call him for many years) offered him articles. He was Bill Foster's first articled clerk, and he was to be paid a wage of £3 per week, at a time when it was normal for principals to demand a capital payment for the grant of articles, with no wages or salary being paid during the five-year period of the articleship.

Mr Foster was an old-fashioned disciplinarian who believed in traditional values. He instilled into Jeremy the concept that the accountant's first and overriding duty was to his client. His favourite expression was 'quick's the word and sharp's the action'. He arrived in his office each day, promptly at nine o'clock, with his bowler hat and rolled umbrella, and would then invariably call for Jeremy to bring in a file on some issue which he had been considering on his way to the office. 'Jeremy,' he would say, in his gruff Lancashire voice, 'bring in the Jones file – and quick's the word and sharp's the action.'

A strong and affectionate bond developed between Jeremy and Mr Foster as Bill Foster became the father whom Jeremy had never had. Shortly after he qualified, Jeremy became a partner in Foster & Co., and five years later, the firm's name was changed. Remarkably, the change was not to the more logical Foster, Stephens, but to Stephens Foster. Bill, as Jeremy now had to remember to call him, had insisted that Jeremy's name was to be the first in the firm's title as, he said, 'You will still be here when I have gone.'

He was, of course, correct. Bill Foster eventually retired and, after only a short illness and at a comparatively early age, he died. His forty-a-day Capstan full-strength ('coffin-nails' to the cognoscenti), cigarette habit had taken its toll. But Stephens Foster prospered. Jeremy was now the senior of eight partners, for he had admitted others into the firm to cope with the expansion of the practice. The expansion, however, had been carefully controlled as he had developed the firm in accord with the guiding principles laid down by Bill Foster. In particular, on the singular importance of the client. 'The client is king' could have been the contemporary slogan.

Soon after he was made a partner, Jeremy married Alison, a girl he met in the local Young Liberals Association. Alison had a typical, conventional but happy, Home Counties background. Her father was a doctor, and her mother a full-time homemaker and enthusiastic supporter of good causes. There were two sons, but both had left home some years earlier and were now living and working abroad. One had emigrated to Australia after following his grandfather's example and qualifying as a doctor and the other was in New York, working on Wall Street. Home for Jeremy and Alison was a large (now too large) family house in Godalming, where they led a comfortable middle-class life. They were members of the local golf club, with Alison being the better player.

In the strange way in which some people grow into looking exactly like their name would suggest, Jeremy had developed from the awkward Manchester schoolboy into somebody who looked as if he could well be called Jeremy. He had matured into a stereotype of the layman's idea of an accountant. He was a cautious, soft-spoken man, whose Lancashire accent, without any obvious effort on Jeremy's part, had long since disappeared, apart from the occasional lapse into flattened vowel sounds, which would make clear his origins to the more acute and discerning ear. He wore heavy horn-rimmed spectacles, had a friendly face despite its usually half-guarded expression and, although he did not quite have a ready smile, when it did break through, it was warm and genuine. He invariably wore, as he did today, a conservatively cut, charcoal-grey suit with a white shirt and sober tie. The traditional, professional accountant's uniform was completed with highly polished black leather, laced-up shoes.

He had been successful by the standards of most people, particularly given his working-class Rochdale background and his unsettled childhood. He was proud of what had been achieved at Stephens Foster, and of the values that he had helped to establish. But he was no longer enjoying his work. He had gradually become disenchanted with an accountancy profession which had changed beyond recognition since he had qualified nearly 40 years ago. But before Jeremy's daydreams about his increasing disillusion could develop into the melancholia to which he had recently become prone, he was interrupted by a message to the effect that Mark Palmer would be a little late, but was on his way. Jeremy's thoughts then came back to Mark and the meeting with the bank, which was shortly to begin.

David Palmer's family business had been one of the first audits on which Jeremy had been engaged as an articled clerk. David was the first person whom he could remember meeting who was Jewish. In Manchester there were Protestants and Catholics, but he had not been aware of meeting any Jews. Although he had remembered that in his grandmother's Manchester home anybody who was particularly inquisitive was accused of being a 'nosey Cohen'. It was an expression which he might have casually used himself without being aware of its provenance and its anti-Semitic implications. There was, of course, a large Jewish community in Manchester, although even here there was division, with those Jews who lived in North Manchester rarely mixing with those who lived in South Manchester. But Jeremy, at the time, knew none of this.

Jeremy and David Palmer immediately hit it off. David, though tough and frugal in his business life, was warm and generous in his personal relationships. Jeremy had watched with admiration as Mark's father had painstakingly developed the business in the austere post-war years. He liked to think that in a small way his advice had been helpful, particularly in the later years, in establishing the business on such a sound financial footing. But, in the decade since David's death, he had not been able to exercise the same influence. He had stood by helplessly as Mark pursued some of his more madcap schemes. Mark did not like interference or opposing views; and he had a foul temper. The foundations of the business, which had taken almost 50 years to build, were quickly undermined. And Jeremy was nauseated by Mark's dissolute lifestyle.

At which point any further reflections were cut short as Mark entered the room, but, this time, without his normal bombast. It was a much more subdued Mark.

Chiswells had been established in the late 1960s – a relative new boy in a City steeped in history and tradition. It had run into difficulties in the financial 'melt-down' of 1974 and 1975 when property prices – on which much of its lending had been secured – had suffered a fall in values of between one third and one half; but, against all the odds, it had survived. It had recently built up a reputation as a specialist in advising smaller companies.

Chiswells' chairman, Alan Copeland, came from a provincial background, he was born and went to school and university in Leeds, and had been a corporate lawyer before moving into merchant banking. He was a tall, overweight, heavily jowled figure with black, curly thinning hair. Many people had found it difficult to understand how he had become so successful – because Chiswells had prospered greatly under his chairmanship – but he had concentrated on cultivating those whom he had considered important to his future, and he had been ruthless in dropping those who were no longer helpful to him. He was respected by most of those who did not know him, but was despised by many of those who knew him well.

Alan Copeland had entered the room with his easy smile already in place and with the reassuring squeeze of his firm grip. But merchant bankers never travel – or attend meetings – alone. With the chairman were Richard Potter, the corporate finance director (almost everybody, thought Jeremy, seemed to be a director in a merchant bank), who had acted for Palmer Industries on the previous transaction, and a more junior executive – still, he had the title of assistant director – who was to take the notes of the meeting.

Jeremy was invited to speak first and he outlined the problems which faced, separately, Palmer Industries and Mark Palmer. He emphasised the need to raise fresh capital, both for the company and for its shareholders. He explained that Mark's preferred route was for a stock market flotation but that they were now here to listen to whatever advice Chiswells had to offer. Jeremy was careful not to allow his own views to influence his presentation. Chiswells had been supplied, before the meeting, with copies of Palmer's most recent accounts, financial expectations for the current year, projections for the next year and cash flow forecasts. Alan Copeland referred to these figures in his response.

He spoke flatteringly of the strong position which Palmer's original business still occupied within its industry and of the high regard in which it was held. But then he came to the heart of the matter. 'The acquisitions have clearly not been successful. They have spoiled the otherwise impressive profit record and they are a continuing drain on the company's cash resources.' Turning to Mark, he said, 'They have been a diversion and, inevitably, it has stretched your management. In an ideal world, and given sufficient time, it would be better to dispose of the unsuccessful acquisitions, return to the core business and then have a company which just might appeal to the stock market. However, there are two problems with that approach. Firstly, you have said that time is of the essence – you need to raise money quickly. Secondly,' and here he carefully sought words which he hoped would not cause offence, 'it might be difficult to persuade investors that they should back a management which had made those unfortunate acquisitions.'

Alan said that he did not believe that it was possible to organise a stock market flotation within any reasonable time scale. Mark then intervened and half-heartedly mentioned the meeting with Michael Fisher about venture capital finance. This time Richard Potter responded. 'We do have a small in-house venture capital fund but it concentrates entirely on management buy-outs.' Exactly the same approach as that of Michael Fisher, Mark reflected ruefully.

Alan resumed, 'We have discussed your problems internally before this meeting,' he said smoothly, 'and we do not think that venture capital is the answer. We believe that the only way to meet your objectives – particularly bearing in mind the timing requirements – is a trade sale. There are a number of companies which we believe we could interest in the idea of acquiring Palmer, and our view is that it is the best, if not the only, solution.'

Mark looked crestfallen, while Jeremy avoided his gaze for fear of presenting an appearance which might suggest, 'I told you so'. Jeremy eventually looked towards Mark, and then spoke for both of them. 'I think that we will need some time to consider what you have said, and then we will come back to you.'

As they rose to leave, Alan asked Mark, almost as an after-thought, whether, should he decide to go ahead, and if they were able to find a buyer, he would want to carry on working in the business. Mark was distressed. He was disappointed at the outcome of the meeting. However, after several moments' delay, he spoke, awkwardly. 'I haven't really thought about it but I'm sure that I will still need to earn a salary. I can't just live on the capital and I have no other way of making a living.' He sounded dejected. Alan, however, seemed oblivious to this and responded cheerfully. 'Well, that's good to know because a buyer might well make continuity of management a condition of any deal.'

Mark and Jeremy shared a taxi from the City back to Regent's Park. Mark was deep in thought as he contemplated the possible consequences of selling Palmer Industries to some other company. He had become used to doing things in his own style and to getting his own way. For more than ten years now, since his father's death, he had felt answerable to no one. And he had exploited the opportunities of this privileged position to the full. Many of his personal expenses had been met by the company. The lack of his father's clear sense of business morality had made it difficult for him to draw a line between his business activities and his personal life.

The company had been his plaything, which he had used to indulge his fantasies and to finance his lifestyle. Even Mark realised that this arrangement would not withstand a moment's objective scrutiny by any third party. He felt helpless, as if he was losing control of his life, and he no longer had the energy to reassert himself. His preoccupation with Jane, although this had not established itself so clearly in his own consciousness, was a distraction from his apparently insoluble business problems, an escape mechanism.

Eventually, he turned towards Jeremy. 'Well, you've been vindicated. There seems to be no alternative to a sale.' Jeremy remained silent and Mark, hesitantly, asked how a takeover would be likely to affect his independence.

Jeremy tried to make a helpful, but realistic, response. 'Much will depend on the type of company that makes the acquisition. A company already engaged in similar markets to Palmer – perhaps producing competitive products – will most likely be looking for the benefits of rationalisation – lower costs and fewer jobs, with perhaps the possibility of integrating two or more factories. In those circumstances the loss of independence could be severe. On the other hand, if the acquiring company is a more diversified group with no activities in the same line of business as Palmer, then it should be possible to retain a greater degree of independence. Either way,' Jeremy felt obliged to make clear, 'it will be inevitable that more disciplined financial and managerial controls will be introduced and, of course, you will be answerable to some other person – the chairman or chief executive of the new owner.'

Mark did not respond. As the taxi drew up in Regent's Park, he then said to Jeremy, 'You had better get on to Chiswells and tell them to go ahead. We seem to have no other choice. But tell them that I will not be sold to a competitor. They must find a buyer who will still need me to run the business. And tell them to get a move on. We need to act quickly.'

Jeremy continued in the taxi towards his own office – and to carry out his new instructions.

CHAPTER NINE

Alan Copeland was standing alone in his high, spacious office admiring the spectacular views of St Paul's Cathedral. He was reflecting on the Palmer Industries meeting, and on the subsequent telephone call from Jeremy Stephens. Work had already started on the preparation of the sale prospectus, but it would be two weeks before it was completed. He thought that it might speed things up if he were to telephone, on a no-names basis, the advisers of those companies that were known to have a particular appetite for acquisitions. He walked back to his desk and set to work. Inevitably, Tudor Holdings was on the list and he was soon speaking to the director at Gresham's Bank who handled the Tudor account.

He was pleasantly surprised at the friendly response to the call. James Gordon usually adopted a rather superior attitude in his dealings with those he saw as being only minor players in the City – and he would certainly have placed Chiswells in that category. However, today he was unusually receptive and, after hearing a number of the salient features of Chiswells' client, he asked for a written summary – still on a no-names basis – which he could discuss with his client.

Mark Palmer was in a mood of confused and nervous excitement as he drove from his office in Regent's Park and turned into Baker Street. It was only a week since his meeting at Chiswells, and work on the sale prospectus had hardly begun, yet he was now going to a meeting with Gerald Howard, the chairman of Tudor Holdings. The pace at which events had moved had left him slightly dazed. Although Mark had said to Jeremy that they should get on with things, he could not easily understand the need for such dramatic urgency. Tudor had responded positively to the preliminary information memorandum they had received from Chiswells. Mark had then given permission for the name of Palmer Industries to be disclosed. The same day he had been asked to attend a meeting with Gerald Howard at Tudor's offices.

Apparently Howard thought that personal chemistry was important and wanted a meeting before speculating time and money on any further review or investigation. He had insisted that the meeting be held at his office, without merchant bankers, and that it be confined to just the two principals. Mark had been reluctant to meet Howard alone and it had been conceded that Jeremy could accompany him. Mark was aware of Howard's reputation as a tough negotiator, a ruthless cost-cutter, and a highly successful businessman, and he was determined to have his accountant's comforting presence by his side.

As he crossed Oxford Street and turned into Green Street, the excitement grew – but so did his apprehension. Although he had been convinced that a trade sale was now inevitable to re-establish his finances and to enable him to repay his debts, he had never thought that things would progress so quickly. Now he was about to meet a man who could change his life, irrevocably.

From what Mark had heard of Gerald Howard he knew that he would not make an easy task-master. Yet he must sell. He really did not have any alternative.

He turned left into Park Lane and accelerated smoothly. All the traffic lights were green. Perhaps, thought Mark, this was a good omen. Having negotiated Hyde Park Corner, he moved into Knightsbridge and approached Tudor's offices, just before the Berkeley Hotel. A uniformed security guard stepped out, as arranged, to take care of the car. Mark handed over the keys and wondered what the future might hold for his beloved Porsche. He would make sure that it was covered in the discussions. Jeremy was waiting for him in the reception area.

*

The three men sat with their coffee at a small side table by the window of Gerald Howard's office, looking out over Hyde Park. Gerald and Mark had greeted each other warily and were now conducting a stilted and guarded conversation about the splendour of the views into the park, the glories of an unseasonably warm May, and holiday plans.

Gerald saw sitting opposite to him a loud, brash, spoiled playboy. While Mark saw facing him a man who fitted perfectly Aneurin Bevan's description of Hugh Gaitskell as, 'a cold, dessicated calculating machine'.

Jeremy sat quietly observing the proceedings with some distaste. He was under no illusions about Mark but, so far as Gerald Howard was concerned, he detested him and all that he stood for. He did not create or produce anything but was simply a master at juggling figures and at slick presentation. He certainly did not create jobs, as redundancies inevitably followed in his wake; and any apparent wealth creation was illusory, depending on the vagaries of the stock market rather than on any underlying fundamentals. Truly, thought Jeremy, a product of the candy-floss culture. He could not see the point of the man.

The initial signs had not been auspicious, but Gerald was now going out of his way to be affable. The temperature had slowly thawed. Mark explained why it was that he and his sisters were contemplating a sale. He made it clear that he wished to continue in his role in the business under a prospective new owner. He talked about Palmer Industries' products and the markets in which they operated. He stumbled a little in trying to explain the philosophy behind the ill-fated diversification programme and its responsibility for the high bank borrowings. Gerald, surprisingly, did not press him on this or any other matter. What did interest Gerald were the financial accounts. Palmer's financial year ran to the end of March and, as it was now the middle of May, Gerald was anxious to know the status of the audit.

Jeremy was able to confirm that the audit was virtually complete and that it had not thrown up any problems. The meeting did not last much longer. Gerald seemed impatient to conclude matters and to move on to other things, and Mark was only too pleased for the meeting to end and so avoid the risk of any seriously probing questions. They both agreed that the meeting had gone well and that they would speak to their respective financial advisers – their merchant banks – to decide what should happen next.

As Mark drove back to Regent's Park, he reflected on the fact that Gerald Howard had not asked him about Palmer's head office, which any new owner would surely want to axe, and he had not mentioned the car. Perhaps, thought Mark, Gerald was not as bad, or as sharp, as he had been painted. At which point, Mark determined to put these issues to the back of his mind. He was going to see Jane again. This time in New York. A prospect which immediately cheered him up. Perhaps everything was going to work out all right after all.

'That man is an absolute shit,' said Jeremy, using an expletive which was rare for him, and even rarer when in conversation with his wife. It was towards the end of a late supper with Alison in their Godalming home, and Jeremy was voicing the frustrations of the day and, in particular, of his first meeting with Gerald Howard.

'It is easy to be cynical about that kind of person, but impossible to be cynical enough,' he exploded. 'He was smooth and smarmy today, but that shouldn't fool anybody. I don't trust the man.' Alison diplomatically steered the conversation in a different direction. She mentioned the current political situation and referred to a television interview with Shirley Williams, which Jeremy had missed. It proved to be a mistake.

Jeremy was proud to be the chairman of his constituency's Liberal Democrats. But, having been a lifelong Liberal, he was becoming as disenchanted with politics as he was with his profession. True to his Lancashire roots, he was an old-fashioned Liberal. He believed that governments do most things badly, and should do less. He was concerned at the extent to which what he described as the 'SDP elements' had assumed dominance since the merger of the SDP and the old Liberal Party in 1988. The Social Democrats had been very much the junior partner at the time of the merger, but its leading members now occupied most of the key party positions, and many had been made peers of the realm.

'Shirley Williams!' he now exclaimed. 'How my own party can deify that woman, as they do, and actually elevate *her* into the House of Lords, I do not know. I hold her personally responsible for the destruction of secondary education in Britain. I see every day of the week at the office the pitiful output from our state schools: school-leavers uneducated in the basic skills of reading and writing, and unable to perform simple adding and subtracting tasks without the aid of a calculator. The direct result of a spiteful act of misdirected class warfare,' he concluded, with long-winded eloquence.

Alison ventured to suggest that no political party seemed to have a sensible policy on education. They all seemed to want to spend more on a failed system. 'Absolutely right,' said Jeremy. 'And it is not only education. It would not be possible today to slide a cigarette paper between the political views of the leader of our own party and those of the leader of the Labour Party. They might both be social democrats, whatever that might mean, but the one thing of which I am certain is that they are not liberals. Interfering, tax-and-spend meddlers, who still think that the man-in-Whitehall knows best, is how I would describe them,' he fumed.

Alison had hardly uttered a word. Her attempt to find a topic that would have enabled Jeremy to unwind from the pressures of his day had badly misfired. She got up quietly from the table to clear away the supper dishes and to prepare for bed.

CHAPTER TEN

Meanwhile, Mark was preparing for his trip to New York. Mark had only rarely been to America. Palmer Industries' business activities were mainly confined to Britain, and what little export business did exist was in Europe. So there had been little opportunity for long-distance overseas travel on business matters. And Mark's vacations were invariably spent at his favoured resorts in Switzerland and France. Palmer's did, however, import much of its manufacturing machinery from overseas suppliers, and was currently in the market for a new, expensive knitting machine. Its purchase would normally have been left by Mark to his production director, but it now provided him with the necessary excuse for his visit to New York. A fictitious meeting with the head of an American engineering company enabled him to justify his absence from home to Gail and, of equal importance, to charge the expenses to the company.

The cost of Concorde he then justified as being necessary so that he would be away from home for only one night (and back in time for one of Gail's fabled dinner parties), and away from his desk and the developing negotiations on the business sale for just two days. When he had discussed with Jane his latest 'incredible idea' of the tryst in New York, he had asked about hotels. 'You must stay at the Carlyle,' she had said, 'it is really, really classy.' And that was where he had booked his room.

Mark then had his first experience of apparently arriving at his destination before his departure. Concorde left Heathrow at half past ten, and arrived at JFK at half past nine local time. Mark's taxi, having negotiated the inevitably heavy traffic through Queens, deposited him at the junction of Madison Avenue and 76th Street a little before eleven o'clock. The doorman escorted him to the reception desk with the quiet courtesy which was the hotel's hallmark and, as he checked in, he could almost feel the aura of its old-rich clientele which seemed to be visibly hanging in the air. He was taken to his room on the 32nd floor in the manually operated elevator with white-gloved, practised efficiency.

As soon as he was alone, Mark telephoned Jane at her office in mid-town Manhattan. 'Darling, I've arrived. I'm in the hotel. When can you get here?'

'Steady, I'm still working,' she replied.

His howl of protest was quickly smothered as she laughed and said, 'But only for another hour! Look, honey,' she continued, 'we will have to eat some time, so I've booked a restaurant for lunch at twelve o'clock – we all eat early here – it is the Café des Artistes, which is on the west side of the park. You can walk there, the concierge will tell you how. It will be good for you. It is sunny, but we still have low humidity, and it's not too warm,' she said, displaying a practical side to her nature of which Mark had until now been unaware.

Mark showered quickly and then reported to the concierge, who gave him a map of the walks in Central Park – although Mark saw that it was intended primarily for joggers – and he was waiting at the restaurant when Jane arrived, a little late. She looked stunning in her smart grey business suit, and within minutes of her being seated, Mark's impatient and restless hands were soon busy under the cover of the long tablecloth. Jane tried to calm him down by getting him to concentrate on the wine list, but he would not be distracted and said that she should order.

'Well,' she said to Mark, with the waiter now hovering by the table, 'as you are now in America, I think that we should choose a Californian wine.' Turning to the waiter, she said, 'We will have a bottle of Mondavi fumé blanc.'

Before the waiter could move away, Mark now swiftly intervened. 'And we want to order the food at the same time,' he said sharply, almost rudely, 'we are in a hurry.'

After lunch, Jane wanted to walk back to the Carlyle, retracing Mark's steps through Central Park, but Mark was insistent that they should get a taxi. 'But honey,' said Jane in a teasing and frivolous mood, 'there is a zoo in the park and it would be fun to visit.'

'If I want to go to a bloody zoo,' said Mark, 'I can go at home, in Regent's Park.' With which he promptly hailed the taxi, which was then passing in the street by the restaurant.

Mark and Jane were soon in their room at the Carlyle and this time their love-making began in a more conventional style – on the super-king-sized bed which was the centrepiece of the room. But it was no less urgent and immediate. The afternoon was spent in luxurious, hedonistic euphoria. However, during a rare lull, when Mark's energy appeared to be flagging, Jane told him of her latest experiences on the slopes. The previous weekend, she said, she had spent in Utah, where the season ended later than in the other ski resorts, stretching into May.

'I was with Estelle, skiing in that dry, light snow which is at its best in the late spring in Utah. Just like icing sugar. As we cut through the snow, it was rising so that we were literally breathing in the powder. It was so exhilarating. Then, d'you know what we did?'

'No,' said Mark drowsily, only half-listening.

'Well,' said Jane, undeterred, 'there was hardly anyone else on the mountain. It was really hot – 65 degrees – so we both took off our shirts and our bras and we skied all the way down, through the deep powder, topless.' A disclosure that quickly re-aroused Mark's interest, which perhaps had been Jane's intention.

Jane, eventually, was the first to move away from the bed. It was already nightfall. She went to the window to look at the view down Madison Avenue and called for Mark to join her. 'Just look at those lights, darling,' she said, 'isn't it absolutely magical?'

From the great height of their room, and the hotel's northerly position, they could see the whole of the skyline of downtown Manhattan. It was a forest of lights, with the tall buildings giving the appearance of giant candles sitting on the most enormous birthday cake. The unbroken line of car head and tail lights seemed like a long, undulating, luminescent caterpillar crawling its way up

Madison Avenue. They heard only a gentle hum from the traffic and the occasional, half-smothered honk of a taxi-horn in the lofty eminence of their 32nd floor eyrie. Suddenly, both at the same time, they were aware of a ravenous hunger. But this time for food.

'Honey,' said Jane, 'let's go and have supper, and listen to Bobby Short.'

'Bobby who?'

'Don't be stupid, darling. You must have heard of Bobby Short. He is a very well-known cabaret artist. In fact, I thought that he must be dead, but it says on the card on the dressing table that he's performing downstairs at the Café Carlyle. We can eat while we are entertained. It should be fun. And,' she added, as a clincher, 'very romantic.'

Mark realised that this would almost certainly mean a later night than he had hoped for. And it would be unlikely that there would be much sleep once they did get to bed. He had to leave the hotel by half past six the following morning to catch his Concorde flight back to London so that he would be home in time for Gail's dinner party. And the next day, he suddenly remembered with some irritation, he had a meeting arranged with lawyers on the sale negotiations. He was going to be very tired. But he turned to Jane, kissed her fully on the lips and said, 'Why not?'

CHAPTER ELEVEN

Two weeks after the meeting with Gerald Howard, Mark and Jeremy were again at Chiswells together in one of the bank's larger meeting rooms. Also present were Chiswells' corporate finance director Richard Potter, and his assistant, a partner from Palmer's solicitors, who also had an assistant with him, the audit manager from Stephens Foster, and Nigel Kendal, who was Palmer's finance director. Alan Copeland had been on hand to greet everybody on arrival and had promised to return again later – no doubt to shake hands at departure time.

Nigel Kendal, who was rarely seen without a cigarette between his lips, qualified as an accountant with Stephens Foster and had worked on the Palmer audit. When it became clear that he would not be invited to become a partner at Stephens Foster – he had not been thought to be partner material – Mark's father recruited him to join Palmer's as finance director. He had performed a worthy, if unimaginative, job and, although he had intended to stay just a few years while gaining experience in industry, his lack of any further ambition or initiative had meant that he had not moved on. He had a unique experience and knowledge of Palmer's affairs over a long period and Jeremy Stephens and his firm's audit manager placed great reliance upon him.

Richard Potter took charge of the meeting. 'Good morning, everybody,' he said jovially, 'we have work to do. Although we have agreed, in principle, the price which Tudor will pay for the acquisition of Palmer Industries, there are still two major obstacles to overcome. The first issue is that Tudor wants its own auditors to examine Palmer's accounts. This is a perfectly normal requirement and, in fact, what Tudor is proposing is a much more modest investigation than is usual in these matters. The suggestion is that Tudor's auditors will carry out what is described as a "limited review", and that this will be completed within a week.'

It was agreed that this should not present any problem, and Nigel Kendal and Stephens Foster's audit manager, who would be the two people most involved on Palmer's side in the investigation, both said that they would make themselves totally available. Jeremy remarked that he couldn't see that very much would be achieved in a week's work, and that there were inherent risks in tight schedules, and unrealistic deadlines.

'I don't know why,' he complained, 'that these things have to be carried out in such an unseemly rush.' However, he had then reflected, Tudor was calling the shots and the risks that were being taken were with its money. Mark, also, was bemused at the speed of everything. Shortly after his return from New York, with surprisingly little haggling, agreement had quickly been reached on the price that Tudor was prepared to offer. Mark had, in any event, not been of a mind for detailed and protracted negotiations.

The value which Tudor had placed on the Palmer business was £15 million, to be satisfied by the issues of new shares in Tudor. It was at this point in Mark's meditations that Richard introduced the second major condition of the deal. 'Tudor has stipulated that 80 per cent of the £15 million of Tudor shares has to be retained by the Palmer vendors, Mark and his two sisters, for at least one year.' There had been intense discussion in the past few days in an attempt to vary this condition, but to no avail. Tudor had insisted that the vendors enter into formal undertakings not to sell £12 million of the Tudor shares for twelve months. The remaining £3 million of the consideration would be in cash, which Tudor would raise by placing a sufficient number of its shares through the stock market with financial institutions. Mark and his sisters had finally agreed to this restriction with extreme reluctance; without it, there would be no deal. And, however anxious Gerald Howard seemed to be to buy Palmer, he had correctly judged that Mark was equally keen to sell.

On completion, each of the Palmer siblings would receive £1 million in cash. There would be capital gains tax to pay and, so far as Mark was concerned, the remaining balance would not even pay off all of his borrowings. However, there would be enhanced dividends on the new Tudor shares which were to be retained, and, in a year's time, more of the shares could be sold. Also, he had been able to negotiate a new two-year service contract at his existing salary of £250,000 a year, and, although the lavish level of his expense account could not be maintained, he was to retain the Porsche. So Mark, after weary hesitation, looked towards Jeremy, then at Richard, and confirmed that the condition was acceptable.

The final matter to be discussed was the timetable. Richard again held centre stage. 'The size of the transaction is below the level prescribed in the Stock Exchange listing undertaking, so that it is not necessary for Tudor to obtain the prior approval of its shareholders. Tudor plans to instruct its lawyers to prepare contracts at the same time as the accountants' review is taking place so that both can progress in parallel. All this will save time, so the provisional plan is for completion and announcement in just seven days.'

So long as nothing goes wrong, thought Jeremy. And much still needed to be done.

CHAPTER TWELVE

Jeremy drove home to Godalming deep in thought, in a mixed mood and a mildly agitated state of mind, late on the evening of the meeting at Chiswells on the Palmer sale. It really did look as if the sale was going to go ahead. Tudor seemed keen to buy – indecently so, thought Jeremy. And Mark Palmer had to sell. It was the only way out of his financial problems. It was a pity that such a small proportion of the purchase price was to be satisfied in cash, and that there were restrictions on the sale of the shares in Tudor. But Jeremy understood the reasons.

He knew that it was not an unusual requirement in transactions of this nature, where an owner-managed private company was being sold to a public corporation. Nonetheless, Jeremy had still had his reservations. Mark would be locked into (without an exit, at least for a year) a company which he no longer controlled. But Mark had been impatient for the deal to be completed, and had seemed unusually preoccupied and so, with some continuing personal doubts, Jeremy had reluctantly recommended to Mark that he should accept.

Of course, if the deal did go through, Stephens Foster would lose Palmer Industries as a client as its accounts would then be audited by the auditors of Tudor Holdings. Although its loss would be a blow, Jeremy was not particularly despondent on that front for he had not enjoyed the audit in recent years, and he could certainly cope with the prospect of seeing less of Mark Palmer. The problem was that the loss of an audit client to one of the big battalions was not an isolated event. It was now part of a trend and the changes in the profession that had brought about Jeremy's disillusionment.

He remembered with nostalgia the early distant days when he had first worked with Bill Foster. Relationships with clients were closer and cosier. It was almost unheard of for a client to leave one accounting firm for another. Long-term relationships had literally been lifelong; and they had usually been social as well as business. Clients had also been friends, and business discussions had as often taken place on the golf course, or in the local Conservative or Liberal club, as in the office.

Today, it seemed to Jeremy, the profession had been taken over by marketing men obsessed only with size and market share. He did not believe that it was any longer clear that the accountant's first responsibility was to his client. Expansion, and the next deal, were the issues. And poaching, which would have been a professional and social kiss of death 30 years ago, was now the order of the day. Bill Foster would be turning in his grave, thought Jeremy.

The major firms of accountants now competed ferociously with each other and targeted particularly the smaller firms such as Stephens Foster. As Jeremy knew from bitter personal experience, they would submit a below-cost fee proposal for the audit – 'low-ball' was the jargon – and once they had their foot in the door, they would push their specialist and consultancy services on which they made high margins as a way of recouping the losses on the audit fee. And merchant banks now routinely advised their clients that, if they wanted to improve their credit rating and obtain the highest stock market basis of valuation, their accounts should be audited by one of the top accountants. The end result was that the top five accounting firms were now themselves large scale, international financial conglomerates; they were bigger than all but their very largest clients.

Jeremy reflected, not for the first time, that it no longer seemed like a profession. He believed that these massive financial super-markets created unavoidable conflicts of interest and that clients were better served when auditors were purely auditors.

And then there were the new accounting standards which, thought Jeremy, seemed to change almost daily and which, he also thought, made accounts more complex rather than more easy to understand. Jeremy had believed, since his earliest days with Bill Foster, that accounting was an art rather than a science and that common sense and sound judgement were the prerequisites for a good auditor. He did not approve of the proliferation of technical committees and discussion papers; and he thought it stupid to attempt to treat every company as if it were ICI, with a 'one-size-fits-all' approach. Jeremy was convinced that clients, and particularly their shareholders, were being short-changed by the new commercialism. He believed that audits were not as thorough as they used to be, and that too many auditors were prepared to cut corners, both to save costs and to pander to the profit-performance requirements of their clients' finance directors. He would point, by way of evidence, to the dramatic rise in litigation costs over allegedly negligent audits; and to the five-fold increase in his own firm's professional indemnity insurance premiums – 'to help pay for the mistakes of others', as he had put it.

At this point in his meditations Jeremy drew up on the gravel drive outside his home. But his mood had not improved.

CHAPTER THIRTEEN

Sarah Armstrong had been a strong advocate of Tudor Holdings, both in her previous position and after her arrival at RAM, and her funds were Tudor's largest shareholder. Tudor did not conform to the profile of many of RAM's more recent successful investments, as it could not be further removed from the new technology which were their distinguishing feature. However, Sarah had, from the outset, been impressed by Gerald Howard's self-confidence and zeal, and she had been amply rewarded for the maintenance of her early support.

Sarah had been informed of the proposed acquisition of Palmer Industries by Tudor towards the end of May and she had readily agreed to buy the shares, which were to be placed through the stock market to finance the cash element of the deal. It would consolidate RAM's position as Tudor's major shareholder, although this was now very much small beer in the context of RAM's hugely increased business.

In any event, Sarah was more concerned with a deterioration in RAM's recent performance – the 'blip' was being prolonged – and at the first hint of incipient internal dissent. In the final quarter of the previous year – Sarah's third full year with RAM – her funds had been near the bottom of the performance tables, the stock market had continued to stutter, and the high-flying stocks to which RAM was so heavily committed had shown further falls. Fortunately, the strong performance in the first three-quarters meant that for the year as a whole RAM was still close to the top of the table. But it was no longer number one.

To add to Sarah's woes, the so-called 'value investors', those fund managers who had stuck to traditional methods and who had long been regarded – at least by Sarah and her colleagues – as the dinosaurs of the investment world, had replaced RAM at the top of the final quarter's tables. The value investors had been sceptical of the supposed 'new economy' and they had refused to join in the chase to push the prices of shares in the over-hyped, cash-hungry companies that made no profits and owned no assets to higher and higher levels. As the shares in these companies had continued to defy gravity, the value investors were derided by the financial press for their over-cautious approach, were constantly described as being old-fashioned and fuddy-duddy, and they had languished at the bottom of the performance tables. They had also lost business to their more bellicose competitors. Now, at least in the short term, there appeared to have been a reversal of fortunes. And those who worked in the City were judged and lived and died in the short term.

Matters came to a head at an unusually long session of one of Sarah's early morning meetings. The comparative figures for the first quarter of the current year had just been received and RAM had under-performed against the stock market indices by more than four percentage points. Robert Price, one of Sarah's senior colleagues, a dark brooding presence who had been at RAM longer than Sarah and who might have had hopes for her job before her arrival, asked the first innocuous-sounding question.

'What will the house line be on our performance and policy when the regular round of meetings with trustees starts in a couple of weeks' time?' he asked of Sarah. A director of RAM and the relevant portfolio manager made a quarterly presentation to the trustees of each of the funds under management (usually a pension fund), the director to explain the overall RAM strategy, and the manager to report on the performance of the specific fund.

'We must stress the positive,' replied Sarah, briskly. 'We were top of the performance tables in two of the past three years and fourth in the third year. Taking the three years together, we are easily number one, and we have significantly out-performed the indices. The short-term correction to the stock market' – she avoided the word 'blip' – 'was bound to have a greater affect on a more aggressive investor such as RAM, but when the Stock Market resumes its longer-term upwards trend – and we believe that it will – then our funds will be the beneficiaries.'

'But what about future policy?' Robert gently persisted.

'It remains unchanged,' said Sarah. 'It has been highly successful in the past and we see no reason to change a winning formula.'

Another manager, a tall, slim, flat-chested woman, known by her male colleagues as 'back-to-front', chipped in. 'But more and more people are beginning to question stock market valuations, particularly of some of our core holdings which, despite the recent fall, are still historically high.'

'Well, those people just do not understand,' Sarah replied. 'We have entered an era of low interest rates and low inflation and we also have the impact of the new technology which has transformed the nature of markets and of expectations. The old bases of valuation are simply obsolete.'

'What about the threat of a recession?' asked a fourth member of the group.

'I don't buy that either,' said Sarah, 'and mainly for the same reasons. And if you read Anatole Kaletsky in *The Times* today you will see that he agrees with me. He believes that there will be a "soft landing", with the avoidance of recession in America and a slight slow-down to a more modest level of growth in the UK.'

'Well, people always say that it is different this time round,' said Robert. 'I think that we might have a tougher time with trustees than you are anticipating.'

One of Sarah's younger and more thoughtful colleagues intervened. 'I accept that, on the back of our longer-term success, we might just be able to sell the idea of the merits of the continuity of our investment approach,' he said. 'But I suspect that we might have a problem with the trustees of a small but still significant number of the funds that we manage. The fact is that there is a wide divergence in performance from fund to fund within the overall total. Some funds have produced results which are seriously below our overall average; a far greater variance than would normally be tolerated with modern management techniques. I think that it is in this area that we might run into trouble. Perhaps we should review our procedures. We could bring in a specialist consultant to make recommendations on systems for risk control.'

Sarah's colour was now rising. She was not used to such outspoken challenges to her authority. Which was how she perceived this unwanted suggestion.

'Incompetent and indecisive managers bring in consultants as an exercise in backside covering,' she said. 'We are paid – and very well paid – to use our own expertise and judgement in deciding what our policies and procedures should be and I have no intention of bringing in consultants who will waste our time and the company's money.'

Her colleague responded more meekly. 'Sorry, it just seemed to me that the people we employ are, by their very nature, more inclined to look for growth opportunities than to seek to avoid risk and that it might be an issue.'

As Sarah gathered her papers together to indicate that the meeting was now at an end, Robert made a final comment. 'Well, let's hope that you are right, Sarah, and that it is just a blip.' Which did little to improve her mood.

CHAPTER FOURTEEN

Sarah arrived home that evening, late and weary. As she turned the key and opened the front door, the twins rushed into her arms like over-excited puppies. 'Mummy!' they squealed, in unison. 'We've been waiting and waiting. Daddy said we could stay up until you came home – but then he said you were going to be too late – but now here you are. Please, please, Mummy, can we stay up with you for another half hour?' with one twin starting and the other finishing each sentence.

Sarah felt the familiar pangs of guilt at the fact that she did not spend nearly enough time with her baby girls. And at six years old they were no longer babies. She carried them into the nursery, where they had been watching television, switched the set off and then sat down with them, one on either side, each snuggled under a protective arm. She encouraged them to tell her about their day at school, but within five minutes it was clear that they were more than ready for their delayed bedtime. They were already in their night clothes and Sarah carried them up the staircase – exclaiming to them at the burden of their growing weight – carefully tucked them in, and kissed them goodnight. Simon had already been through his ritual of the twins' final hugs and kisses, so Sarah now went back downstairs to join him in the library, where he was waiting with her glass of champagne already poured.

Sarah rarely drank with lunch and this was her first drink of the day. It was a time which she savoured and a moment to which she looked forward at the more stressful times of the day. They talked about the progress that the twins were making at school. How quickly they were growing up. How excited they were at having been allowed to wait for Sarah's arrival. After the first glass, they drank a little more champagne before moving into the kitchen, where the housekeeper had prepared supper.

The housekeeper had simple tastes and cooking was not one of Simon's strengths, so the offering of plainly grilled lamb cutlets was not very ambitious, but Simon had more than compensated for the modesty of the food with the extravagance of the wine. And wine was definitely Simon's territory. One of his projects, when he had stopped working full time in the City, had been building and stocking a wine cellar with all the gadgets for controlling temperature and humidity, and he now had an inventory of more than 2,000 bottles. It consisted mainly of white wines from Burgundy and red wines from Bordeaux. Simon would not claim to be an expert, but he now knew enough about the wines of these regions to have bought shrewdly and, most importantly, claret and white burgundy were the wines which best suited their palates. They knew what they liked. He had experimented a little with wines from the New World, particularly Chile, Australia and California, and he had developed a taste for Château Musar from the Lebanon, but here, he relied more on the advice of others. And usually he would quickly return to his first loves from France.

Tonight he had chosen a bottle of Château Lynch Bage 1970 to accompany the lamb. It had been one of his early purchases, more than ten years ago, when it had cost no more than ten pounds a bottle. Now, the cost of a wine of similar quality would be ten times that amount and, despite his wife's millions, Simon baulked at paying these prices. Still, that was a thought far from his mind as they took unreserved pleasure from the first taste of this most delicious of clarets.

After the initial 'ooh's' and 'ah's' over the quality of the wine, Sarah blurted out what had been on her mind throughout the drive home. 'That bastard Robert Price has never forgiven me for taking the job which he thought belonged to him. And he can't stand the fact that he has to report to a woman.'

'What's happened this time?' said Simon. It was not the first occasion on which this subject had been raised.

'Well, you know the situation in the markets. You know that we are not doing so well. Nothing surprising in any of that. But he keeps niggling. And today I actually think that he put somebody up to suggest that we bring in consultants to advise on risk-management techniques. How bloody ridiculous. That's supposed to be *our* job.'

'So what are you going to do?' said Simon.

'Business as usual. It's just a blip,' as this phrase slipped out, Sarah paused with a wry smile. 'I must stop saying that. It's almost becoming a joke in the office. Anyway, as soon as the markets recover, we will be back at the top again and I am not going to be panicked into unnecessary changes.'

'But what if markets don't recover – the situation in the oil industry is going from bad to worse? And wasn't it Keynes who said, "If circumstances change, then I change my view"?'

Simon's reference to the oil industry brought about a sharp shift in tack. 'Sorry, always obsessed with my own problems. What's your news? I had seen that the oil price is still depressed.'

'That's the issue. The price continues to fall. Exploration companies have all cut back on new drillings, and there is no work around. I haven't had a new assignment for more than two months, and prospects have never appeared bleaker. Who wants to hire a consultant when the oil companies are all laying off their own people?'

'Darling, I am sorry, but you mustn't worry. We have more than enough money, you're fantastic with the twins and something will turn up eventually.'

'But I do worry. Looking after the house is just not enough and the twins now spend most of the day at school. I was wondering whether I should look for a proper job in the City again.'

'Simon,' said Sarah, now suddenly concerned, 'please, not now. I'm not sure that I could cope with the pressures at work and the disruption to the domestic routine which that would entail. Please, leave it for the moment.'

And there, for the moment, it rested.

PART TWO: CONSEQUENCES

CHAPTER FIFTEEN

Tom Curtis was sitting at his desk at the *Financial Times* when the news of the Tudor Holdings takeover of Palmer Industries appeared on his screen. It was early on a Friday morning and it looked like being the first really hot day of the summer. Tom had been musing on his plans for the weekend, which included taking part in a cricket match – he was an off-spin bowler – but the news item had brought him back swiftly to the present. For Tudor Holdings was one of the companies that Tom followed, in his job as a financial journalist, with a deeply sceptical eye. As he read Tudor's official press release and came across words such as 'synergy' and phrases such as 'long-term investment', his cynicism grew. He wondered what the real reason for the deal might be. Tom believed that Tudor had passed its 'sell-by date'. It had continued to make acquisitions in unrelated fields when that fashion had long disappeared and it was difficult to see that Tudor had actually improved any of the businesses it had bought. Furthermore, and Tom believed this to be crucial, when there was an increasing desire for more transparency in business affairs, the opaque nature of Tudor's accounts and official statements went very much against the grain.

Tom called an analyst at Tudor's stockbrokers to share his doubts, but the analyst sought to reassure him, saying that it was a relatively small transaction which was of no great consequence. 'A bolt-on acquisition' was the phrase that he used.

Tom wrote a short, slightly querulous piece for the Saturday paper, which questioned the logic of the specific acquisition and doubted the wisdom of the overall strategy. Tudor should be selling companies, not buying them, was his conclusion. But he knew that his would be a lone voice in the wilderness. The rest of the media would take the official company line and the supposedly serious Sunday newspapers would have been fed background information to support the usual anodyne, flattering profiles. The timing of the press release for a Friday would help to ensure maximum coverage in the Sunday papers. And the *Financial Times*, which was the only paper likely to be critical, happened to have its smallest circulation for its Saturday edition. All part of the Tudor strategy, thought Tom.

CHAPTER SIXTEEN

Gerald Howard and Anthony Kemp were together for their usual morning meeting. It was the week after the completion of the Palmer takeover. Gerald was looking more relaxed than he had seemed for some months. And Anthony was preening himself on meeting the tight timetable. The final contracts had actually been signed at four o'clock on the Friday morning. Anthony had complained that lawyers seemed to believe that they always had to run completion meetings into the early hours to justify their large fees.

There was now a mood of mutual self-congratulation. It seemed that, with the inclusion of Palmer's suitably massaged profits, Tudor could just about meet the profit expectations of the City. It was now early July and Tudor's financial year ran to the end of September. This meant that three months of Palmer's figures could be included within Tudor's. But Anthony was confident that, with his imaginative approach to accounting matters, he could present Palmer's accounts in such a way as to show no better than a break-even position for the first quarter of its accounting year, so that the whole of its half-year profits would be pushed into the second quarter. These profits would then be added to Tudor's figures.

Anthony had cautioned that this adjustment might require Mark Palmer's co-operation and that it was vital to keep him on side. Gerald said that Mark was an idiot, but had agreed that they needed to keep him sweet for the moment, and that no major changes should be made at Palmer until after the year-end and the finalisation of the accounts.

The remaining issue that Gerald and Anthony had touched upon was the press and City reaction to the news of the deal. The City response had been fairly muted and, as Tom Curtis had predicted, the media comment was generally bland and uncritical with most papers simply printing verbatim extracts from Tudor's press release, and the Sundays the usual eulogised personality-based pieces, with Gerald as the hero. None of this, however, registered at all with Gerald, for he was obsessively concerned with the one newspaper, the *Financial Times*, which had not taken the 'official' line. He became agitated as he re-read the offending article.

'How,' he enquired of Anthony, 'can a journalist' – a 'bloody teenage scribbler' he called him, which was neither original nor accurate, 'write in such an insolent and ill-informed manner? And why do our financial public relations people still allow it to happen? They are supposed to control these things.'

As his agitation grew, he called his secretary into his office and told her to speak to Tudor's PR company and to get its chairman in for a meeting before the day was out.

Gerald knew from personal experience (it had often worked to his advantage) that the quality of financial journalism was not always high, and that many of those who wrote the copy were not noted for excessive energy; nor were they highly paid – at least compared to the rewards which were available elsewhere in the City. He had seen the development of a new breed of financial public relations consultants who had been quick to seize the obvious opportunity. They could guarantee for their clients acres of uncritical 'comment' in return for easy access, exclusivity, and generous entertaining. Tudor's own PR company had been created by one of the brighter and more ambitious journalists who had crossed over into this lucrative world of public relations.

Five years earlier, Giles Sutton had left his job as deputy city editor of one of the Sunday broadsheets to form Sutton Communications, a 'boutique', specialist financial public relations consultancy. He had deliberately kept his client list short and concentrated on the type of client who might have had a difficult image if it had not been for Giles Sutton's assiduous use of his tickets for Glyndebourne and the Royal Opera House and his special tables at Mark's Club and Harry's Bar. No expense was spared when Giles was spending his clients' money in maintaining the friendship and support of his Fleet Street contacts.

He was an expert in the black arts of his trade and was particularly adept in his use of the 'Friday drop'. This was a procedure whereby market-sensitive information was 'dropped' to favoured journalists on a Friday night, in time for exclusive coverage in the Sunday papers, before its formal release into the public domain through the normal stock exchange channels on the Monday morning. It was a widely used technique, which the regulatory authorities had signally failed to stop and in which the Sunday broadsheets were eager participants. And, of course, the favours were expected to be reciprocated.

Giles was now with Gerald, a client of two years' standing. They were sitting, in the late afternoon sunlight, at the same side table occupied not so long ago by Mark Palmer and Jeremy Stephens. Giles had brought with him Rebecca Shaw, who was the executive who handled the Tudor account on a day-to-day basis. They were discussing the *Financial Times*.

They were all very much aware that the *Financial Times* was read each working day by virtually everybody in the City and in the business community. Although the financial pages of other newspapers had a wider general readership, there was no comparison in terms of influence. Profiles and designer photographs in the *Sunday Times* might massage the ego, but it was the *Financial Times* that was taken seriously by those people who really mattered.

Gerald had complained bitterly that, despite having paid a retainer of £50,000 to Sutton Communications in each of the past two years, as well as untold expenses, there had been no softening of the hostile tone of this crucial newspaper. Giles had felt aggrieved that Gerald held little regard for the generous and complimentary coverage in the rest of the media, but Gerald had reminded him that the reason for his appointment had been to deal specifically with the *Financial Times*.

'The key issue,' said Giles, 'is Tom Curtis. The problem,' Giles continued, 'is that Curtis still does not understand,' (not trust, he almost said), 'Tudor Holdings or Gerald Howard. He has resisted all offers of hospitality. He seems determined to maintain his distance. When I suggested lunch at Le Gavroche to talk things over he was disdainful and almost contemptuous. He was bloody rude.'

Rebecca then spoke for the first time. She was conscious of Curtis's role as a senior and highly regarded writer at the *Financial Times*. He had a much wider and more versatile role than the typical company news reporter, and she saw his by-line in different parts of the paper as well as being attached to the occasional feature article in its Saturday edition. He seemed to have been following the progress of Tudor Holdings for a number of years and was invariably the author of the critical articles on its affairs, even to the extent of writing, on one occasion, a lofty paragraph in the news-paper's mighty Lex column.

'It is obvious,' she now said, 'that Tom Curtis has no time for public relations people. But, what if Gerald were himself to offer an exclusive, in-depth interview to Curtis? I know,' she said to Gerald, 'that normally you never do this, but its very originality could be the attraction to Curtis. And if successful, it might disarm him and make him less prejudiced against our cause.'

Gerald had a policy of not giving any interviews that might be considered serious. He was notoriously thin-skinned and disliked being challenged. He was happy to give 'soft' background to saccharine profile writers but, for anything more demanding, he preferred to deal through Sutton Communications. However, it was clear that this policy was not working with Tom Curtis, and Gerald gave serious thought to Rebecca's suggestion. The situation, he knew, could not get very much worse, and it just might help.

Giles was initially more cautious. He had seen how quickly Gerald could lose his temper if things were not going his way – he had often borne the brunt of it himself – and he was fearful as to how Gerald might respond to a persistent and aggressive line of questioning by Tom Curtis. Much would depend upon the setting. Which was when Rebecca had her brainwave. She knew that Gerald was due to leave the following week for his summer holiday in the South of France. She also knew that work always constituted part of his holiday plans.

She said to Gerald, 'Why not invite Tom Curtis to join you at your holiday hotel for the interview? It will be much more relaxed for both of you. And when Curtis sees the extent to which you have gone to accommodate him, and in a holiday environment, he might well lower his guard. It must increase the chances of a favourable outcome.'

Gerald was interested and turned to Giles. 'Would Curtis be able to accept such an invitation? Would the *Financial Times* allow it?'

Giles knew that in his previous incarnation as a financial journalist on a Sunday newspaper he would have jumped at such an offer. But the *Financial Times* would have a tighter regime. 'It's likely that the paper will have fairly strict rules about the kind of hospitality that its staff can accept. It will need to be proportionate to the value of the news story to the paper. However,' he said carefully, 'the fact that it would have exclusivity, and knowing that you do not normally offer such interviews, and given the level of its interest in Tudor, it could well satisfy that test. It might just work.'

That was all that Gerald needed to hear to convince him that they should make an approach. Rebecca was given the task of speaking to Tom Curtis to sound him out.

CHAPTER SEVENTEEN

Tom Curtis was on the telephone to his publisher. His first novel was currently with the printers and had a publication date in early September. He was checking with the publicity department the arrangements for its promotion and the publicity manager, Fiona, was transferring his call to a colleague who was going to handle his book and whom she had described as 'our new recruit'. The new recruit came to the telephone and introduced herself as Sally.

'I am told that you are new,' Tom said.

'Yes,' Sally replied, 'this is my first day here.'

'Where were you before?'

'Nowhere, this is my first day at work.'

'You mean, your first job ever?'

She did. Where else but in publishing, he reflected, would the launch of a new product be placed in the hands of the newest of raw recruits?

Tom's book concerned big business and the City. It had seemed to him, from his perspective as a financial commentator, that there were few good novels with a business background. He believed that businessmen generally did not write particularly well and that professional writers usually did not know enough about business. He had persuaded a publisher friend that there was, indeed, a gap in the market and the result was this first novel. The experience of writing it had convinced him that his initial analysis had been accurate. Although he knew far more about business than most writers of fiction, he had found it difficult to get inside the minds of his business characters and to convey credibly their motivation. This was something which he was determined to improve upon for his next book, on which he had already started work.

The call from Rebecca was, therefore, particularly opportune. He was taken aback initially at such an unusual approach on behalf of a company whose chairman had, until now, taken such pains to avoid confrontation and who had left the media – certainly, the *Financial Times* – very much to his aides. It was, for Tudor, a high-risk proposal and he was intrigued as to what might lie behind it. However, it took little to persuade him that he should quickly grasp this unique chance of an exclusive interview with such a controversial and slightly mysterious businessman as Gerald Howard and to have such prolonged exposure to him in his own setting. As one of its more senior reporters, he had been able to persuade the higher echelons at the *Financial Times* that it was a worthwhile project and he had been able to fit the trip into his work schedule, although it would mean missing an important cricket match. He was also looking forward to meeting Rebecca Shaw, whom he had not met before. She had sounded bright and lively on the telephone. He was to fly from Heathrow to Nice and she had already sent his ticket – club class.

She was to meet him at Nice airport.

CHAPTER EIGHTEEN

Tom Curtis had started with the *Financial Times* as a trainee eight years earlier as one of its limited intake of graduates straight from university. He was now thirty-two, about five feet ten inches tall, with a slightly built spare frame, a round, even-featured face and mousey-coloured hair, cut fashionably short. The overall impression was of a neat, fairly serious person who would not stand out in a crowd. However, the exception to this otherwise nondescript appearance was his eyes. They were green with flecks of hazel and they were clear and challenging and strong. They suggested that it could be a mistake to underestimate Tom Curtis.

As he stepped onto the tarmac at Nice airport, Tom was hit by the heat and the light. He had left London on an early morning flight on a grey, cold, wet and miserable day that was more typical of February than July. The contrast now could not have been greater and, although he was wearing the casual clothes which were his invariable attire, it was soon obvious to him that he was overdressed.

He passed through customs, where he was greeted by Rebecca Shaw. He was immediately struck by her appearance. She was tall, almost his height, with long dark hair, deep brown eyes and a wide calm flat face which brought to his mind the painting of the Mona Lisa. He guessed that she was in her mid-twenties. Although she had been on the coast for only two days, she was already lightly tanned – her skin, unlike Tom's, was of the kind that quickly and easily took the sun. And her short sundress showed off her brown and long slim legs to maximum effect. She had a soft voice and welcomed him in a light and amused manner, which Tom found disturbingly seductive. He had to remind himself that he was embarked on a serious business trip, not a vacation.

Rebecca had a cabriolet parked just outside the air terminal. As she drove out of the airport car park, she took the road away from Nice and followed the signs for Cannes. She described the route which they were about to take to Tom.

'We will travel along the autoroute, but before we reach Cannes, we will take the exit for Antibes. Then we will drive through the old town of Antibes, past the ramparts and take the coastal road to the Hôtel du Cap at Cap d'Antibes. It should take just a little longer than half an hour.'

She explained that she would be responsible for looking after him during his stay and she discussed with him the likely itinerary.

'Gerald Howard's normal routine is to play tennis with one of the hotel professionals for an hour at eight in the morning and again at six in the evening. It is far too hot to play during the day. He will then spend some time working in his suite and reading by the pool, although he rarely settles long in any one place. He is very restless,' she exclaimed, as she turned to look towards Tom and caught his direct gaze.

She quickly turned her attention back to the road. 'Usually, he has lunch at the hotel but goes out for dinner, sometimes with friends. There are many special restaurants set in the hills and along the coast. I am sure that you will see one of them. He is with his wife, but she keeps very much in the background.

'Gerald has planned your interview for the afternoon – after lunch; how about half past two in Gerald's rooms?' she suggested.

'Fine,' Tom nodded.

'Gerald would like you to join him and his wife for dinner this evening. I am also invited,' again, casting a coy glance in his direction. 'Tomorrow,' she said, this time looking more directly towards him and with laughter in her voice, 'is your free day. You can stay around the hotel and enjoy its facilities – there's a fabulous swimming pool among the rocks – or you can go sightseeing. I will be around to look after you, as required, and I will deliver you back to the airport at Nice in the evening,' she concluded, with a final mischievous smile.

As Rebecca chatted, Tom became more and more relaxed as he adjusted to the new environment. Only three hours ago he had been in the London drizzle. The soft top of the convertible motor car was open to the skies so that they were fully exposed to the sun and the air. He felt intoxicated with the wind in his face, the sun on his back and with the air strongly scented from the white oleander and purple bougainvillaea which lined the road. Not to mention the presence of Rebecca, who was sitting in such close proximity in her small car.

As they approached Cap d'Antibes, he looked across the bay towards the heat-haze hanging over the sea in the middle distance. They followed a bend in the road. And then he saw the hotel. The Hôtel du Cap was one of the world's most exclusive hotels. It was also one of the most expensive. Its name was not to be found in the usual brochures which listed fashionable and luxury hotels, for it was literally in a class of its own. Set in parkland, on a promontory with the sea on three sides, and situated at the most southerly tip of Cap d'Antibes, it was in one of the few remaining unspoiled parts of the South of France. As Tom and Rebecca entered the marble entrance hall they could see, through the open doors across the hall, the long walkway which led, through carefully manicured and constantly watered gardens, to the appropriately named Pavillon Eden Roc at the very edge of the sea. It had an air of peace and tranquillity and great luxury, in total contrast to the noise and crowds and bustle of the surrounding holiday towns and beaches.

Tom's room was in the annexe – a long, low, elegant white-painted building about 50 yards from the main hotel. His was one of the more modest rooms but he saw, from the room rates listed on the card which was hanging inside the wardrobe, that the cost for just one night was still more than he would normally spend on a complete week's holiday. And the price for the room did not include breakfast. As Tom unpacked his overnight bag, he realised, with a start, that allowing for the one hour time difference from London, it was, here in France, already one o'clock and he was due to see Gerald Howard in one and a half hour's time. He ordered a sandwich from room service and settled down to review his notes and to prepare for the interview. He had almost lost sight of the fact that this was why he was here.

Gerald Howard's suite was on the first floor, in the centre of the main hotel building, looking out towards the Mediterranean. Tom had approached it in a gilded glass-sided lift cage and had just met Gerald for the first time. They were now facing each other in comfortable armchairs sipping iced water. Rebecca was also there, sitting to one side. The windows and doors to the balcony were closed against the heat and the efficient air-conditioning system meant that the air was satisfactorily cool.

Tom had not seen Gerald in the flesh before, although he had, of course, seen his photograph many times in the newspapers and had watched him once on television. He did not usually attend company annual general meetings, where Gerald would be obliged to make an appearance, as they tended to be stage-managed and it was rare for any new information to be disclosed. Tom did attend press briefings at results time but Gerald left those to his finance director and his chief executive. So, despite the fact that Tom had been writing about Tudor for several years, he had not previously met its chairman and driving force.

Gerald was now wearing a short-sleeved shirt, loose-fitting trousers and casual shoes without socks. The effects of the sun had given a healthy glow to his appearance but Tom's eyes could not avoid being drawn to the sharp pointed nose that gave him such an over-eager look and to the incongruous nature of the impossibly unfashionable hairstyle. He had greeted Tom with apparent enthusiasm and they were immediately on first-name terms. As they engaged in small talk before settling down to the serious business of the meeting, Tom thought that Gerald spoke just a little too quickly, and he judged that beneath the forced bonhomie there was more than a hint of nervousness and uncertainty.

Before the arrangements for the interview had been finally agreed, there had been some to-ing and fro-ing between Rebecca – on behalf of Gerald – and Tom as to how wide-ranging the discussion would be. Initially, Rebecca had suggested that Tom should submit a list of proposed questions that he would put to Gerald, but Tom had rejected that out of hand. He had made it clear that the only way he could justify the project was if there were to be no restrictions of any kind. No business subject was to be off-limits so far as his questioning was concerned, he had stipulated. And that was what was agreed.

Tom asked Gerald his first question, 'Can you define the purpose of a company such as Tudor, which is engaged in so many different activities in such disparate fields?'

Gerald responded pompously, 'Tudor's mission, the very reason for its existence, is to increase shareholder value and this is achieved by delivering an improvement in earnings per share on a consistent basis, year by year.'

Tom asked, 'How can this be brought about? Why should it not be possible for each of the individual subsidiaries to do at least as well as separate independent businesses rather than as a part of a sprawling conglomerate?'

'Superior management,' was Gerald's quick response. 'In fact,' Gerald said, warming to his subject, 'the business of management – or the management of businesses – is what Tudor is about.'

'So, it doesn't matter what the business is, whether in manufacturing or retailing, in food or engineering, the approach is the same?'

'Absolutely. We apply our management techniques to improve the underlying performance of each of the individual businesses.'

'You make it sound very easy, but is it not just a variation on Jim Slater's simplistic and now discredited statement of 30 years ago that, "we don't make things, we make money"?'

'The answer to that is in our results. In each of the past twelve years we have increased our overall profits and our earnings per share and that is the acid test of success in business.'

'But,' Tom persisted, 'doesn't your approach lead to short-termism? You acquire a new company, reduce its head office costs, slash its marketing and research and development budgets, and starve it of new capital investment. It might increase profits in the short term but it is a trick that you can only perform once and, in the long term, the business will surely stagnate.'

Gerald brushed this to one side by repeating, 'Just look at our results,' and by pointing to the counter cyclical value of a broad spread of interests. 'It is the opposite of having all your eggs in one basket,' he said.

Tom changed tack slightly. 'One of the problems we have in analysing Tudor's results and judging its performance is that comparisons are made difficult by acquisitions and by changes in accounting policy.' At the mention of accounting policies, Gerald bristled, began to redden, even through the sun tan, and showed the first signs of irritation. 'Our accounts are audited by one of the top accounting firms,' he blustered, 'and our accounting policies are no different from those adopted by other similar companies.'

Tom moved on to the balance sheet and to cash flow. It was obvious that Gerald knew his way around all the figures in the accounts, but when it suited him, he pleaded ignorance. 'I am not the finance director,' he would say.

Tom was left without a satisfactory answer to his question. 'If the business is so profitable, why is it not generating more cash?' The figures, thought Tom, did not quite add up.

Tom's questioning had, until now, been fairly gentle. He wanted to coax as much information as possible out of Gerald without antagonising somebody who had a reputation for having such a short fuse. But, as the interview neared its end, he became a little more waspish.

'If the key to Tudor's success is the quality of its management, why is it that it is perceived as being a one-man band, with you as executive chairman exercising total autocratic control? Surely the best managers would not work for such an employer.'

Gerald was stung by this and rose to his feet. As he answered, he strode round the room, clearly agitated. 'Each of our subsidiaries has its own managing director, who is highly motivated, with an incentive plan which pays cash bonuses based on his own subsidiary's performance, and with share options in Tudor. The managing directors report to the group chief executive, who is based in Tudor's head office. At the head office, apart from myself and the group chief executive there is also the finance director and the three of us form the executive committee, which is responsible for overall strategy. So it is nonsense,' he concluded, 'to talk of a one-man band.'

The temperature of the meeting had changed. The warmth and enthusiasm of the initial welcome had evaporated and, as the interview was concluded, Tom was coldly reminded that he was expected for dinner that evening.

Tom was having a simple continental breakfast in the already hot sun on the hotel terrace as he reflected on yesterday's events. The interview, from Tom's point of view, had gone tolerably well and he thought that he would be able to write a worthwhile piece for the paper, although he felt certain that it would not be entirely to the satisfaction of Gerald Howard. The dinner had been a mistake. They had dined at the Restaurant Bacon, which was just a ten-minute drive along the coast, and they had enjoyed a delicious bouillabaisse, which was Bacon's speciality. The conversation, however, had been difficult and stilted. Gerald's wife had seemed to have absolutely nothing to contribute and Gerald himself did not have very much to say outside of business. Tom had been thankful that Rebecca had been there, in fact, more than thankful. The more he saw of Rebecca, the more intrigued he was. She was a very attractive woman. And despite Tom's deep and long-held prejudice against people employed in public relations, he had to recognise that she was also serious and intelligent. It was clearly her job to look after him and to make him feel cared for, and she had certainly succeeded in that. Tom hoped that her interest might be a little more than just professional. He was to meet her in half an hour's time, at nine o'clock, when they were to go together into the town of Antibes and then return to the hotel for lunch. She was later to drive him to the airport in time for the evening flight.

Tom and Rebecca spent the morning like any other tourists. They drove along the coastal road, passed the restaurant at which they had dined the previous evening and then, after entering Antibes itself, they took the narrow road at the edge of the sea, which was flanked by the Mediterranean on one side and the old walls of the town on the other. They passed the old port with its wide array of fishing boats and the strong smell of the sea and then came to the Port Vauban, where hardly a patch of water was to be seen between the massed ranks of yachts of every size.

They parked their car in the market place and from there they toured the narrow winding streets of the old town. Some were so narrow that they could hardly walk by each other's side and, as their eyes were drawn towards the narrow rectangle of sky, they could see at the higher levels of the tall buildings, washing hanging from lines strung across the street.

Tom insisted that they stop for coffee at the restaurant which had been Graham Greene's (one of Tom's heroes) favourite haunt before they returned to the car and set off for the hotel and lunch. He felt as if he had been on holiday for a week.

The terrace at the restaurant at Pavillon Eden Roc overhangs the Mediterranean with views of the sea in all directions. Everything is white, from the white marble floor, white pillars, white painted tables with crisp white linen to the white sun umbrellas adjacent to each of the tables. It all shines brilliantly and dazzlingly in the bright sunshine. Rebecca had made a provisional booking two days earlier in the hope that they might lunch there, which had proved fortunate as every other table was now occupied. Tom and Rebecca each had a glass of champagne to start and both ordered the same food: a tomato salad followed by plain grilled dourade royale with olive oil and lemon. Rebecca asked Tom to choose the wine and, to cloak his unfamiliarity with the extensive list, he quickly chose a bottle which he recognised from the Bacon dinner, Domaines Ott, a dry white wine from Provence.

They chatted over lunch like old friends with any remaining inhibitions falling away as a result of the effects of a combination of wine and sun. He talked about his cricket and the subtleties of off-spin bowling (he played regularly on Hampstead Heath) and his writing. He explained to her that one of the attractions of the interview with Gerald Howard was that it might help him in his fiction writing, as well as providing a story for the *Financial Times*.

She talked of her interest in opera and in bridge – he had been right to detect a serious side to her nature. She said that she realised how fortunate she was to have access to Glyndebourne and Covent Garden through her job, although she also supported the smaller productions at more modest theatres and country houses. She loved to play bridge and was a member of the Andrew Robson Bridge Club at Parsons Green – Rebecca lived nearby, just by Hurlingham, while Tom lived in Primrose Hill – but, Rebecca complained that she never had the time to develop her game as she would like.

As they finished their food, Tom noticed a large ocean-going yacht weighing anchor some way from the coast. A motor launch then sped from the yacht with about half a dozen passengers and crew and tied up at a jetty, just below the restaurant, where two men waited to receive them. One of the passengers was separated from the rest and stood on the prow. He looked very debonair, in his spotlessly white trousers and dark blue, open necked, short-sleeved shirt.

As Tom, and now Rebecca, observed the scene, one of the welcoming party on the jetty stretched out his hand to help the first of the passengers – the white-trousered one – off the launch and onto the jetty. The passenger clasped the helping hand and stepped off, but, instead of reaching dry land, he suddenly disappeared between the launch and the jetty and fell with a splash into the sea.

Rebecca and Tom rushed to the barrier that surrounded the terrace of the restaurant and looked down at the floundering passenger, but, apart from his obvious loss of dignity, he seemed to be uninjured and he was soon clambering up the rocks and being helped, this time with more care, onto the jetty.

Tom and Rebecca returned to their table amidst the general hilarity.

'That must have been quite scary,' said Rebecca, when they had re-settled.

'Suppose so,' said Tom. 'He will first have been frightened, then angry, and is now probably embarrassed.'

They paused for a moment, started their coffee, and then Rebecca, who had been looking thoughtful, said 'I've been here once before – which is why I know my way around. It must have been four years ago. I wasn't staying here, of course, or anywhere that was grand. I was in an apartment, just down the coast at Juan-les-Pins, with two girlfriends – the apartment belonged to the parents of one of them – and I was lucky enough to be invited by a banker client, who was staying here with his wife, to join them for lunch. And I just now had the most extaordinary sense of déjà-vu. Because, while I was having lunch with them, a similar yacht approached the coast and the same launch brought its passengers to disembark at the jetty. On that occasion,' she said, 'there was no accident, but one of the passengers was Tiny Rowland, who you must have come across.' Tom certainly knew about Tiny Rowland.

Tiny Rowland was a businessman of infamous reputation, and was, until shortly before his death a year or two ago, the chairman of Lonrho, a company with its origins in African mining activities, which had developed into a conglomerate whose affairs were always shrouded in an impenetrable fog. He had once, famously, been labelled by Edward Heath, then Britain's prime minister, as 'the unacceptable face of British capitalism'.

One of the elements in Tiny Rowland's colourful career had been his appetite for the pursuit of vendettas. He was known as a single-minded and formidable enemy and had been involved in a bitter and highly public dispute with an Egyptian middle-man turned entrepreneur, Mohamed al-Fayed. Fayed had acquired control of the House of Fraser Group, which owned Harrods, Britain's best known department store. The launchpad for Fayed's bid for control had been a shareholding in House of Fraser, which he had acquired from Lonrho. Rowland had then claimed that he had been duped by Fayed and had commenced a long campaign of vilification.

He had published a series of brilliantly written but scandalous letters which had been sent to thousands of important businessmen, politicians and other opinion formers, and to those prominent in the media. Tom had read them with total fascination and, very much against his better judgement, had formed a sneaking admiration for Rowland and for the sheer power with which he put his case.

Many people took the view that Rowland and Fayed deserved each other. One government minister, who had been called to adjudicate between them, had been known to refer to them as 'a pair of bookends'. Tom took a different view. Having read Tom Bower's books on both Rowland and Fayed, on this particular argument, he was definitely on Rowland's side.

So, Tom needed no introduction from Rebecca to the Tiny Rowland story.

'Well,' said Rebecca, after Tom had made clear to her the extent of his knowledge of Rowland's background, 'I had seen some of the letters about Fayed – they were collector's items, and were passed round all the PR offices – and I agree with you that they were very persuasive – and great reading. So, when I saw that he and his party were at the next table I was keen to meet the man himself, and, as we were about to leave, I asked my banker friend, who knew Rowland, to introduce me. I was a bit tipsy by then.

Well you know how he looked, and what great presence he had. He was sitting opposite a man of similar age – in his seventies – and with two women who were probably their wives. He rose from his chair to his great height, looking very distinguished with his full head of silver-grey hair, and with his bronzed, chiselled features. When I told him how much I had enjoyed reading his letters about Fayed he was all smiles. But then – I really must have been tipsy – I said, "The one thing I never did understand was why you sold the shares in the House of Fraser in the first place." Well, the smile disappeared, his face was like thunder and he replied, before sitting down again, "You cannot have read the letters very carefully." But then, the other people at the table all said in unison, "But Tiny, we never understood that either." It was hilarious.'

'That is really very funny,' said Tom. 'It's a great story. And you asked absolutely the right question. Well, Rowland is now dead. But Fayed is still around.'

As they then left their table to take the short walk through the gardens to the hotel, and left behind them the soothing background noise of the lawn sprinklers, Tom was forced to face up to the reluctant prospect of his imminent departure. He would not find it easy to leave Rebecca at the airport, but he was determined to see her again in London.

CHAPTER NINETEEN

Mark was suffering from a prolonged attack of anticlimax. Since the takeover at the beginning of July, he had experienced a constant state of trepidation. He had not been quite certain as to what might happen after Tudor acquired control of Palmer Industries but he had expected change of some sort. In fact, he had only seen Gerald Howard once since the completion meeting and his message had been that he should simply carry on as before. There was, he had to admit, the irritation of the obnoxious little accountant, Anthony Kemp, Tudor's finance director, who was constantly telephoning to ask for information. But Mark invariably had him transferred to his own finance director, Nigel Kendal.

Still, Mark felt as if he were in some kind of limbo and was possessed by a feeling of uncertainty and insecurity. It seemed as if disaster was about to strike and that this was the lull before the storm. Even the improvement in his own finances had hardly added to his sense of security. This was partly due to the fact that the change had not really been that dramatic. The bank, predictably, had insisted that he reduce his overdraft and this had taken a sizeable chunk out of the £1 million of cash which he had received. Gail had taken the opportunity to go on a spending spree and was behaving as if they had won the national lottery, and Mark had heard that his two previous wives were consulting their lawyers and were re-examining their divorce settlements in the light of what they saw as his new-found riches; on top of which, Jeremy Stephens had counselled that he must put sufficient to one side to provide for a significant capital gains tax liability.

Mark was already anticipating the time, a year ahead, when he would be able to realise some of the remaining £4 million by selling shares in Tudor. And it was this prospect that enabled him to quell the rising tide of panic which increasingly engulfed him in the early hours of the morning.

Mark's summer had been disjointed and disappointing. He and Gail usually went to the south of France for the month of August, where they rented a villa at Mougins. Their friends Paul and Helen would then join them for part of the time. This year, to the intense disappointment of Gail, Mark had not been able to raise any enthusiasm for a holiday where he might easily have come across Gerald Howard. Paul and Helen had been obliged to make other arrangements – but this time at their own expense.

In addition to developing a phobia about Gerald, Mark was also, and this was an extraordinary transformation, reluctant to be away from his office for long periods. He was fearful of the unexpected and the unknown.

Gail had spent much of August at their farmhouse in Hampshire and, in between, had over-compensated for the loss of the Mougins holiday with her shopping expeditions. Mark had spent the week-ends in Hampshire, but most of the week in London.

Since his latest adventure with Jane in New York, Mark's telephone conversations with Jane had eased off to about once or twice a week and he had noticed that she was less quick to return his calls. In the middle of August she came to London on a business trip and, for a short time, Mark again had something pleasurable to which he could look forward. He took her to dinner at Harry's Bar and they danced afterwards at Annabel's, and spent the night together at her St James's hotel. But it lacked the sparkle, excitement and raw lust of the earlier assignations.

Mark's summer limped towards a desultory end. In the late afternoon of the third Thursday in September, however, that ennui was about to be dissipated in a dramatic manner.

CHAPTER TWENTY

The ring of Mark's telephone had interrupted Nigel Kendal's 'confession' almost before it had begun. But Mark had quickly dealt with Gail's questions and Nigel was then able to resume.

'You know,' he said, 'that as a result of the takeover, Tudor's auditors are to supervise the stocktaking which we are to carry out at the end of the month.' Nigel paused for a moment, and lit another cigarette from the only half-smoked stub of the first. 'Mark,' he said, 'they will find discrepancies. The stock has been overvalued.' At this, Mark pushed his chair back as if he were about to rise but Nigel pleaded with him. 'Please, please, let me finish.'

Nigel again drew deeply on his cigarette. 'It all began three years ago. As you know, although the new ventures had not been successful and were losing money, the lingerie business was still very profitable. However, when I came to finalise the accounts at the year end, I realised that the increased discounts which we had been giving to Fraser and Green for higher volumes had been much more significant than I had originally calculated. This meant that the profits were far less than we had previously thought. Then I panicked. I didn't have the courage to come and explain things to you and I was concerned that if the banks were told they might withdraw their loans. So I adjusted the stock values. It was very simple really. I selected a number of key items on the stock sheets and inserted the price per thousand in place of the price per unit.'

Nigel seemed to be gaining strength as his story unfolded. He lit another cigarette as Mark looked at him in stunned silence. 'Of course,' Nigel continued, 'I did have some concern about the auditors. But Stephens Foster trusted me totally. Their audit manager had been trained by me and after so many years of carrying out the same audit, they had become complacent. It wasn't difficult to fool them. It was stupid of me, I know, but I hoped that something would turn up in the future to improve things. Then I could have reversed the stock adjustment and everything would have been fine. But it didn't, and it wasn't. In fact, it got worse. In each of the next two years I had to add to the stock inflation to produce the profit figures which you and the banks were expecting. It had become too easy. And I was too frightened to stop. But when I became aware of the stocktaking procedures that Tudor's auditors are to follow, I realised that the game was up. They are bound to find out.'

As Nigel paused to start yet a further cigarette, Mark could restrain himself no longer. 'How much are we talking about?' he said, thickly.

'Three million pounds,' was Nigel's reply.

'Christ almighty,' Mark exclaimed, 'what a fucking mess.'

Jeremy Stephens had enjoyed a quiet reflective summer. After the conclusion of the mad frenzy of the Palmer's sale to Tudor, with its manic and prolonged completion meeting, he had spent most of the time in his office pleasurably catching up on correspondence and dealing with other clients, whose affairs, for a short time, he had neglected.

He had discussed with his partners the implications of the hole in the firm's finances caused by the loss of the Palmer's fee income, but it was thought that with a small amount of belt tightening, the natural growth in the income from other clients would bridge the gap. He had also raised with his partners the issue of succession, as his own impending retirement now loomed on the horizon. And although he was not yet quite counting the days, it was a prospect that the changes in his profession were leading him to anticipate with growing enthusiasm.

One non-professional diversion in his otherwise tranquil summer was provided by a meeting of Jeremy's local constituency party. The meeting had been called to adopt a prospective parliamentary candidate for the next general election. Jeremy, as usual, took the chair and swiftly ran through the routine business before reaching the main item on the agenda, which was the formal adoption of the prospective candidate. The candidate first made a short speech and spoke about the party's prospects at the election.

'As the Liberal Democrats came second to the Conservatives at the last election, we are now classified as a key seat by the party's hierarchy, and receive special financial and organisational support from Cowley Street. This means that we are obliged to co-ordinate our activities with the centre. It has certain implications. HQ at Cowley Street say that this is a winnable seat. They believe, however, that the only way to ensure success is for us to persuade a sufficient number of Labour voters that in this constituency theirs is a lost cause, and that they should, therefore, vote Liberal Democrat as a way of defeating the "common enemy". Tactical voting,' he concluded, 'is crucial and so is the maintenance of good relations with the local Labour Party.'

Jeremy did not agree with all this cosying up to Labour. So far as he was concerned, *both* the other two parties were the enemy. He made a tetchy response from the chair. 'It is a pity that so much of what we say in the party today is about tactics and organisation. We do not, any longer, seem to discuss policy.'

The candidate was defensive. He said, to Jeremy's further irritation, that at the election the policy emphasis – and this, he said, was a directive from headquarters – would be on local issues. And he added that the success of the tactical voting strategy depended on not saying too much that might upset Labour voters. At the further mention of the Labour Party and of directions from Cowley Street, Jeremy almost lost his temper.

'I have not been an active Liberal for most of my life to settle for such modest ambitions as not upsetting Labour. The Liberal Party used to be a party of ideas and to stand for conviction and principle, and if it had not, it would have been no better than and no different from the other two parties.'

He mentioned health and education as areas in which the basic approach of all three political parties was now identical. 'The only question ever asked,' he said, 'is "Who will spend most?", when it must be obvious to any sensible observer that the state is a high cost and inefficient provider and that there has to be a radical change in ways of financing, and change in methods of provision.' This had developed into a polemic.

Jeremy had rarely spoken with such passion. After the meeting, he went to the bar for the customary nightcap but did not stay long. He set off for the ten-minute walk home still seething. Sometimes the airing of a grievance can help to diminish it, but Jeremy's outburst (which is how it must have seemed) had actually crystallised and consolidated his unhappiness. It had strengthened his resolve to do something about it. By the time he reached home, he had decided that he must write to the party leader and set out his concerns.

Jeremy had met Jamie Kilkenny, the leader of the Liberal Democrats, when he had visited the constituency in its new key seats status, but did not know him well. He, nonetheless, felt that he could write to him on a first-names basis although Jeremy did not himself use first names as freely as was now the fashion. He wrote in what he thought was a restrained, respectful and constructive manner. He raised the specific issues about which he had spoken at the constituency meeting but broadened the subject area into the more general development of party policy. He mentioned the famous Yellow Book of the 1930s, in which writers and political thinkers such as Keynes and Beveridge had put forward their then revolutionary ideas on modern economic theory and its practical implications for government policy, and on proposals for state pensions and an incipient system of social security. He made a tentative suggestion that perhaps the Liberal Democrats could initiate a similar intellectually driven review for the start of the twenty-first century.

It was a long thoughtful letter running to some four pages. Even Jeremy, in his modest way, felt a little pleased with the finished product. He posted the letter to the party leader's office at the House of Commons and awaited a response. This time the act of setting down his thoughts on paper had helped. He felt better.

The main feature of the summer, however, and the highlight of their year, had been the three weeks' golfing holiday which Jeremy and Alison spent together in Portugal. Each year they went to the same hotel, at the same time, and met the same people. This had been their routine for more than twenty years, and a number of those they had met in the early years had since become close friends. They looked forward to their annual reunion with their 'holiday family' and their expectations were rarely disappointed. This year had been no exception.

Jeremy was, therefore, as a consequence of the holiday, in a more than usually relaxed mood when, having been back in his office for several days, he took a telephone call from a highly distressed and hysterical Mark Palmer at five o'clock on the afternoon of the third Thursday in September.

Jeremy listened to Mark's emotional account of Nigel Kendal's revelations without interruption. He then asked several questions to clarify points on which Mark had seemed confused. His advice was firm and unequivocal. Mark must see Gerald Howard without delay and tell him the whole story. Jeremy replaced the telephone receiver and sat alone, lost in thought, for some time. His first reaction on hearing Mark's news had, quite properly, been the interest of his client and in determining what steps Mark now had to take. But, as he considered his own position and that of his firm, he was hit by the full enormity of the situation. How on earth had Stephens Foster allowed this to happen?

Early the next day Mark was following the same route from Regent's Park to Knightsbridge as the one he had taken just four months earlier. He refused to allow his thoughts to dwell on the meeting that he would shortly be starting. As he drove through the steady drizzle, he counted the traffic lights – eight red and three green was the tally. It was not a good sign. He had telephoned Gerald Howard the previous evening and simply told him that he had to see him as soon as possible on a matter of great urgency. Gerald had pressed him for more information but Mark had remained firm and it was agreed that they would meet in Gerald's office at nine o'clock. Mark had slept badly. He had had a sense of foreboding about some impending crisis but had assumed that this feeling was related to the inevitable uncertainty created by the take-over. Nigel Kendal's fraud – because that was what it was – was devastating and totally unexpected. Mark's spirits sank even lower when he saw, on entering Gerald's office, that Anthony Kemp, for whom he was developing an irrational but extreme aversion, was also there. On this occasion there were no preliminary pleasantries and Mark was asked bluntly by Gerald: 'What's the problem?'

Mark recounted the story of Nigel Kendal's confession of the previous afternoon. How he had been told by his finance director of the falsification of the stock valuation and how this had brought about an increase in the reported profits. As he stuttered towards his conclusion, Gerald intervened.

'Cut the crap,' he said coldly. 'We all know what the implications of increasing the stock figures are. It's as old as the hills. You deliberately set up this company for sale by inflating its profits and your second-rate auditors let you get away with it. Well, we will not.'

At this, Mark found it impossible to maintain his composure. He broke into an embarrassing series of uncontrollable sobs. If he thought that this might soften Gerald's response, he was soon proved to be mistaken. Compassion was the last thought in Gerald's mind as he erupted into a ferocious rage. He mounted a violent tirade of abuse against Mark, insisting that he must have been a party to the fraud as it was inconceivable that the finance director would have behaved in such a manner entirely alone and without reward.

Neither was Anthony Kemp spared as the harangue continued. Gerald wanted to know why Tudor's supposedly top-notch auditors, who, he said, had acted under Anthony's direction, had not detected the simple and blatant discrepancies. Anthony replied, in a rising, almost breaking voice, that they had all agreed, in view of the time constraints, that the auditors would carry out only a limited review of Palmer's accounts.

Anthony's explanation was cut short by a torrent of expletives. Turning back to Mark, Gerald spoke more calmly and slowly. 'Anthony will take over immediate responsibility for Palmer's business. He will go back with you now to your office and you will clear your desk and go home.'

Looking directly into Mark's swollen eyes, he now spoke even more slowly, and with menace. 'You will not gain from this. I will personally make sure that you are ruined.'

Mark arrived at his St John's Wood home just before lunch and immediately telephoned Jeremy. He was close to a state of total disintegration. He told Jeremy of the outcome of his meeting with Gerald and he asked what was likely to happen next and what he, Mark, should now do. Jeremy said that he could not be certain of the sequence of events. 'However,' he said, 'I expect that Tudor's first action will be to instruct another firm of accountants to carry out an investigation. Its job will be to establish the facts and, wherever possible, to apportion blame or responsibility. This new firm must have had no previous connection with any of the parties involved so that it has no conflict of interest and can clearly demonstrate its objectivity. Obviously,' he said, 'that rules out Stephens Foster and Tudor's own auditors so, however tiresome it might be, it will mean a third team of accountants poring over Palmer's books.'

Not, Jeremy reflected, that this was any longer a concern of Mark's. He then continued, 'It is also likely that the investigating accountants will be asked to assess the extent of the loss which Tudor has incurred as a result of the fraud so that this may form the basis of a claim against those who are thought to be responsible. The £15 million pounds which Tudor paid for the business was based on Palmer's profitability and it is now clear that those profits have been seriously overstated. If Tudor had been aware of the true profit figure, they would have offered a lower price or they might simply have walked away from the transaction. When the accountants have reported,' Jeremy concluded, 'Tudor's lawyers will use their report to support legal action to recover its losses from the alleged culprits.'

Jeremy's advice to Mark was that he should consult his own solicitors as soon as possible. Jeremy had not mentioned the risk of criminal action for he had thought that it might well have pushed Mark over the brink. That, however, was certainly a further possibility, at least so far as Nigel Kendal was concerned.

Jeremy had been hoping to make an early start to the weekend with the prospect of a late afternoon round of golf but, not for the first time, he now realised that it was a pleasure that would have to be postponed. Having waited through the morning for Mark's telephone call, there were several things that he now had to do. First, he needed to speak to Alan Copeland, for Chiswell's had co-ordinated the Palmer side of the takeover, and had provided the usual merchant banker's comfort letter with regard to Palmer's affairs. He rang Alan's office but was told that the bank's chairman had already left for the weekend. Lucky man, he thought, as he asked for Alan's home telephone number. He was soon talking to Alan, who was enjoying lunch in his garden in Hampstead, and who had some difficulty in hiding his irritation at the interruption.

On hearing Jeremy's news, Alan immediately sought to distance himself from the situation. 'Of course,' he said, 'since the takeover by Tudor, Palmer is, technically, no longer our client. So far as accounting matters are concerned,' he continued, 'that is entirely a matter for the auditors of both companies and is something for which Chiswell's bear no responsibility.'

He expressed his gratitude to Jeremy for keeping him informed but made it quite clear that he thought that that was the end of the matter. Jeremy recollected that he had heard from Mark that Chiswell's had submitted one final bank-breaking bill for its role in the transaction. As, post the take over, the cash for its payment was effectively being provided by Tudor, Mark had had little difficulty in approving the account for settlement. And now, Chiswells was planning to wash its hands of responsibility for any subsequent unpleasant consequences.

Jeremy's next call was to his firm's solicitors and arrangements were made for a meeting to be held on the Monday morning. He then had to speak to their insurers as, under the firm's professional indemnity policy, Stephens Foster had an obligation to inform them of any potential claim at the earliest possible moment. Finally, he had to convene a meeting with his partners for later in the afternoon so that they could be brought fully up-to-date with events. It would be some time before Jeremy could begin his weekend.

114

CHAPTER TWENTY-ONE

The third Thursday in September was also the day of the party for Tom Curtis's book launch. Since the parting at Nice airport in mid-July, Tom had been seeing Rebecca on a regular basis. The day after her return to London – two days after Tom – they had arranged to have dinner and within a week, they were sleeping together. Now they spent as much time with each other as the demands of their jobs would allow, and in all respects they were 'an item'.

An unexpected aspect of their relationship had been the pleasure that they had both enjoyed from sharing each other's interests. Tom had spent an evening with Rebecca at her bridge club. He had not played bridge since university but his enthusiasm for the game had soon been rekindled and, although Rebecca was clearly the superior player, they had planned to take lessons together in the winter. Tom's role in their bridge evening had been confined to that of a kibitzer. Nonetheless, his quick, observant writer's eye had soon detected two universal truths about the typical bridge-club habitué. The first was that he, and it was more usually a man rather than a woman, always complained that, when playing rubber bridge, he was dealt less than average cards, and the second was that they all seemed to think that they were better bridge players than they actually were. It had also seemed to him – and this particular bridge club was probably better than most in this respect – that among the bridge obsessives there was more than the appropriate statistical average of social misfits. Still, despite the risk of the occasional irrational rant from one of the resident misanthropes, Tom had seen how easy it would be to get hooked on the game.

The other game which developed a potential for becoming a shared interest was, of course, cricket. And here, it was Rebecca who was being re-introduced to a sport which she had not followed since her father took her to a Lord's Test Match when she was still at school. She now spent a late summer afternoon with players' wives and girlfriends and other camp followers, watching and cheering Tom's cricket team playing a closely fought match on the Hampstead Heath extension. Tom was clearly the bowling star and seemed to be popular with the rest of the team. He had tried to explain to her some of the aspects of his bowling technique.

'My stock ball is an off-break. This is a ball which, when bowled to a right-handed opponent, pitches outside the off stump and then spins in towards the batsman. Occasionally,' he continued, pedantically, 'I will vary this delivery with a leg break, which is a ball that will pitch on the leg side and then move away to the off. Or, sometimes, I will bowl a ball that goes straight through without deviation.'

He showed a now bemused Rebecca how he placed his fingers round the ball and how he positioned the seam of the ball to achieve the desired movement off the pitch. 'When running up to bowl,' he said, 'I will try to shield the ball from the batsman until the moment of delivery so that the batsman cannot be sure which way the ball will spin.' And it was Tom's skills in the arts of disguise and deception that had made him the side's demon bowler.

After the match the team and its supporters had spent a jolly evening at a nearby pub, where Tom and Rebecca had tipsily agreed that cricketers were a friendlier lot than bridge players, before they left together for Tom's flat in Primrose Hill.

Although Tom and Rebecca seemed equally fulfilled in their leisure activities, the same could not be said of their professional lives. Tom seemed entirely satisfied with the combination of his work on the *Financial Times* and his fiction writing, but Rebecca seemed uneasy when discussing her role in promoting the merits of the likes of Gerald Howard. They had their first row when Tom teased her about prostituting herself in the interests of unprincipled businessmen. She had responded angrily, and when Tom said that it was meant to be a joke, she had replied that it was in very poor taste. But they had soon been reconciled.

Tom's article on Gerald Howard had appeared in the *Financial Times* the week after the interview. Although it was distinctly cool and sceptical on the performance of Tudor Holdings and on Gerald's management style, it was more intellectually driven than the content of the interview material might have suggested. Tom had widened his article to cover the role of conglomerates and their need in the future to be far more open and transparent if they were to be taken seriously for investment purposes. The careful reader, however, was left with the clear impression that Tom did not believe that they had a future.

But Gerald's gamble seemed to have paid off. Tom had treated him more gently than his reputation for fearless investigative journalism might have suggested (Tom had hoped that this had not been influenced by his feelings for Rebecca), and the very fact of such a weighty article in the 'pink paper' had given Gerald an added gravitas.

The build-up to the publication date of Tom's book had not gone well. He had been pressing his publishers for some time to be told the number of copies that they were going to print. They had wanted to defer a decision for as long as possible – or so they told him – and it was only three weeks earlier that he had heard that the print run was going to be for what he considered to be the laughingly small quantity of 3,000.

His publisher, responding to Tom's explosion over the telephone, explained, 'You know, Tom,' he said, 'things have changed now. With modern printing technology and new warehouse systems, we can re-order and reprint quantities of as little as a thousand at a time within seven to fourteen days. The short lead time and a rapid response to computer-generated sales figures,' he enthused, 'will mean that your book should never be out of stock in the warehouse. This is the prudent and businesslike way to support a new author such as yourself while reducing investment in stock and eliminating the risk of large numbers of unsold books,' he concluded.

Things had not worked out quite like that. Advance orders for Tom's book from booksellers and book wholesalers, subscription orders they had called them, had quickly exhausted the small initial stock order. On publication day, the day of the launch party, there were no books in the warehouse and the reprint order was not expected to arrive for several days. Tom was told gleefully by fellow long-suffering authors that, when the new stock did arrive, there would be the usual but inexplicable delays, which seemed to be endemic in book publishing, in getting books out of the warehouse and into the shops. Tom wondered whether the new internet booksellers, such as Amazon, knew about publishers' warehouses.

As a result, with at least one review of his book expected to be featured in the weekend newspapers, many of the bookshops held no stock. A situation, he was later informed by visiting booksellers, that was not at all unusual. The publisher's launch party for Tom's book was, in view of its business background, being held in a bookshop in the heart of the City. Inevitably, Murphy's law came into play as the chosen venue proved to be one of the shops without any of the books. Just minutes before the party was due to start, some minion arrived, clutching a dozen copies that had been scavenged from the publisher's publicity department. In an age of advanced technology and electronic publishing, the books had arrived by hand. Perhaps, mused Tom, it was a practical illustration of just-in-time distribution systems.

Tom thought that the party turned out to be rather a waste of time. He got the impression that publishers gave these parties because they believed that it was something that authors expected of them. But it seemed to have no clear marketing objective. Those from the book trade who attended were fairly junior and none of them, it seemed to him, had any authority actually to place orders for books. Increasingly, so Tom was told, this was something that was carried out by some functionary at head office.

There were one or two people from the media but they were from fringe publications and he did not believe that they could have gleaned anything that was newsworthy. What he wanted were serious reviews and books in the shops!

Tom had been encouraged by his publishers to add the names of his friends to the invitation list and to look upon the occasion as a celebration of his book and his authorship. But, if Tom had been planning a celebration he would have done better than an offering of stale peanuts, disgusting sausages and cheap wine.

Rebecca proved to be the party's one redeeming feature. But even her renowned public relations skills were put to the test in dealing with some of the murkier elements of the book trade and their apparently low alcohol threshold. She was cornered, at an early stage, by a small, squat toad-like figure, who claimed to represent one of the publishing industry's trade magazines. She was struck by the fact that he seemed not to read very much and to know surprisingly little about current titles for one who made his living by writing about the book market. As she eventually sought to escape his clutches, she momentarily brushed against his soft, protruding belly – it felt like making contact with a slug.

Her next encounter was with a self-obsessed, sharply dressed Piccadilly bookseller, who was wearing a garish tie that seemed to Rebecca to be a combination of the Botswana national flag and a British Airways tail fin. He had not the slightest interest in Tom's book and spent the time preening himself and trying to obtain Rebecca's telephone number.

What Rebecca did glean from her random conversations was the real reason for short print runs and 'out-of-stocks' in the shops. 'Books,' said the bookshop manager, 'are all sold to bookshops on sale or return. This means,' her informant said, 'that publishers are reluctant to reprint when a book is out-of-stock in the warehouse for fear of a deluge of returns coming back from the earlier "sales" to bookshops. This system of sale or return is,' he said, 'unique to the book trade.' Rebecca told the story to Tom in a state of disbelief.

When Tom and Rebecca, to their great relief, were able to leave the party, they were both nursing nagging headaches and suffering from mild indigestion. Tom told Rebecca that she should leave financial public relations and move over to public relations in the book trade. 'There is obviously an enormous marketing gap,' he said, 'and you will make your fortune.'

CHAPTER TWENTY-TWO

Jeremy Stephens had spent more of the past three weeks with his lawyers than with his clients. After a partnership meeting, it had been agreed that Jeremy, as senior partner of the practice as well as being the partner responsible for the Palmer audit, would handle the day-to-day involvement with its solicitors, as the full significance of the fraud for Stephens Foster unfolded. A junior partner had been asked to work with Jeremy in dealing with the correspondence, attending the meetings and collating the enormous quantities of paper and files that the lawyers were requesting.

The awesome fury of Gerald Howard's rage had been unleashed through a bombardment of threats, abusive letters and letters before action from the notoriously aggressive law firm that Tudor had appointed to act on its behalf. These had culminated in a formal writ, to which had been attached a detailed statement of claim. The writ demanded the payment of the sum of £10 million. A stomach-churning figure that was already a regular feature in Jeremy's now recurrent nightmares. The statement of claim had set out the reasoning and the calculations that sought to justify the recovery of this amount by Tudor from those whom it held responsible for its loss. And Tudor's lawyers had made it clear that Stephens Foster was at the top of the list.

The figure of £10 million had been arrived at by comparing the profit figures that had appeared in Palmer's accounts with the revised profit figures that had now been produced by the independent investigating accountants. The original profit for

Palmer's final year before the acquisition, audited by Stephens Foster and on which Tudor had based its bid price, was £2 million. The new profit figure was alleged to be a little less than £1 million. More than that, the earlier profit record for Palmer's core business of consistent growth over a number of years had now been transformed into one which, at best, showed no growth at all. So it was argued that although the original growth record supported a relatively high price-earnings ratio, the new flawed record merited a much lower one. The final point was that the assets which had been acquired were £3 million less than had been assumed – there was £3 million less stock.

It was these three factors, the reduced level of profit, the blemished profit record, and the asset shortfall, that Tudor had used to support a reduction in the value of Palmer's business from £15 million to £5 million and to make the demand for the recovery of the £10 million loss which it claimed it had incurred.

On a crisp, dry, late October day, Jeremy assembled all of his partners into a large meeting room for a conference with the litigation partner of the firm's solicitors. There were still only eight partners including Jeremy in Stephens Foster, as Jeremy had sought to maintain the intimate, informal family environment that was in such a contrast to the impersonal bureaucratic monoliths that now dominated his profession. The lawyer was to explain the implications of the litigation for the practice and for each of its partners.

Stephens Foster's solicitors, Fisons, was a small long-established firm which was a little old fashioned, not unlike Stephens Foster itself. It had resisted the blandishments to join a larger grouping and had maintained its reputation as a fair and sensible firm which was loyal to its clients and which gave good advice. Fisons had been horrified at the scale of the hostility and the level of vitriol displayed by the unpleasant firm of City lawyers that had been engaged by Tudor. They were, apparently, specialists in high-profile litigation and there had been some pressure, as the size of the problem became more obvious, from some of the Stephens Foster partners and also from its insurers, to use a similar City law firm with a gun-slinging reputation. Jeremy, however, had remained resolute and they had stuck with their traditional legal advisers.

Fisons' litigation partner, Paul Davis, was a neat, bespectacled man in his mid-thirties, with a well-scrubbed face and a straightforward, no-nonsense manner. He started the meeting by giving a simple guide to the tests which, he said, Tudor would need to satisfy, if it were to be successful in pursuing its action.

'Tudor will need to prove,' he said, 'that representations, that is, statements or claims, were made in the course of negotiation; that Tudor placed reliance on those representations in proceeding with the acquisition; that those making the representations were negligent; that there was a duty of care to Tudor on the part of those making the representations; and finally, it will need to be shown that Tudor has suffered loss. All of these tests will need to be satisfied.'

Paul dealt with the last test first. 'On the basis of the independent accountant's report (the conclusions of which had been largely supported by the recent work done by Stephens Foster), I would not envisage that Tudor would have very much difficulty in proving that it has suffered loss, although there is certainly room for argument on the amount.'

'I will examine the other tests,' Paul continued, 'in the context of the possible targets which Tudor will have identified as candidates for legal action in its attempt to recover whatever loss it is finally determined that it has incurred. Before that, however, I want to discuss the issue of joint and several liability. Assuming that Tudor believes that it could successfully sue a number of parties for its alleged loss,' he said, 'it could pursue one or more of that number for the whole of the amount claimed. Each litigant would be separately liable for the whole of that amount in addition to being jointly liable together with the other litigants. Although,' he added with a mirthless smile, 'we all understand that Tudor cannot recover its loss more than once.'

'If,' he went on, 'Tudor felt that it could more easily recover the whole sum from just one of the parties, then it could proceed on that basis and then, if Tudor proved to be successful, it would be up to that guilty party to seek to recover contributions from those others whom it was thought could be found also to have been negligent and so shared that guilt. To be more specific,' Paul concluded, 'Tudor could simply sue Stephens Foster for the whole £10 million and ignore everyone else. It could depend on how strong it felt its case was against each of the possible litigants and what its chances were of recovery. In that situation, if Stephens Foster lost, it would have to sue others, such as Mark Palmer, for contribution. However, I am running ahead of myself because I want to consider the position of each of the parties in some detail.'

Jeremy Stephens and his colleagues already knew about joint and several liability since it was a feature of partnership law and they were all bound together as partners in Stephens Foster. Nonetheless, Jeremy detected several sharp intakes of breath as his partners listened to Paul Davis's bald statement of its current implications.

Paul now came to his list of likely targets and his view of Tudor's probable tactical approach. He said that he would go through the list in the reverse order of value and attractiveness from Tudor's point of view. 'The first candidate,' he said, 'is Nigel Kendal, Palmer's finance director. In terms of satisfying all of the tests, his is the easiest one of all and he has confessed to the fraud that led directly to Tudor's loss. However, Nigel Kendal is a man of straw. He is without resources and Tudor's lawyers will not waste their time and their client's money in pursuing him. It might well be that the authorities will initiate proceedings in the criminal courts but that will take for ever and, in any event, is not our concern.

'Next, is Chiswells, Palmer's merchant bank. Chiswells supervised the acquisition from Palmer's side of the transaction and, in so far as they issued the normal merchant banker's comfort letter, they made representations on which it could be argued that Tudor had placed some reliance. The comfort letter contained the usual disclaimer of responsibility but,' Paul emphasised, 'it must mean something or what is its point? And, of course, they have charged a very large fee for their services so it would not be unreasonable to expect them to accept some responsibility. However, the duty of care that a merchant bank owes, in these circumstances, to the company which is acquiring its client company has not been sufficiently tested in the courts and it could mean having to establish new legal precedents. It might not be easy,' Paul concluded, 'for Tudor to succeed in any action against Chiswells, and they might well decide that there are more attractive opportunities elsewhere.'

There was a brief interruption with the arrival of coffee but Paul was soon again underway. 'Tudor's own auditors prepared a report on which Tudor clearly relied and they obviously have a duty of care to their client. The only question here is whether they were negligent. They will claim that they were asked to carry out only a *limited review* within a very short time scale. They will argue that within those constraints it is unreasonable to expect them to detect a fraud which had been overlooked by Palmer's own auditors, who would have had much more time and who would have been more familiar with their client's affairs.'

He continued, 'It is not entirely clear from the report of the independent investigating accountants that Tudor will succeed in proving that its own auditors have been negligent, but there is certainly room for doubt. Its auditors' insurers might well be prepared to settle the claim for a relatively modest amount so as to avoid a lengthy and costly court action. And that would certainly suit Tudor's auditors, who will be anxious to preserve their valued long-term relationship with their client.'

Paul took a sip of coffee. 'Now we come to Mark Palmer and his sisters. It will be easier if we deal first with the sisters. They, of course, received £10 million of the £15 million sales proceeds but it is difficult to see how Tudor will be able to recover any of that. The sisters were shareholders of Palmer but not directors; they were not involved directly in the negotiations with Tudor, they made no representations and they cannot possibly be held responsible for the fraud. So it seems to me that the sisters will keep their £10 million although they will still be subject to the restriction on the sale of the Tudor shares.

'The first question to raise about Mark Palmer is how much he knew. Did Nigel Kendal really carry out the fraud alone and unaided, and without Mark's knowledge? Kendal claims that he did and Mark denies having even the slightest suspicion that anything was wrong until Kendal's confession. I am, therefore, assuming for the purposes of this presentation,' Paul continued, 'that Mark was not involved in the fraud. However, the fact that he was ignorant of what was going on does not mean that he should not have known. Mark was the chairman and chief executive. Nigel Kendal worked for him. It will be argued that Mark was negligent in not supervising Kendal more effectively and it will be claimed that had Mark been sufficiently close to the business he would have realised that the balance sheet was showing £3 million of value for stock which did not exist.

'I am sure that Mark, in turn, will say that Stephens Foster should have uncovered the fraud, although that will not absolve him of responsibility. I have little doubt that Tudor will be able to prove that Mark was negligent. As all the other tests are easily satisfied, I would expect that Tudor would be successful in any action it took against Mark Palmer.'

As Paul paused to gain his second wind, he refilled his coffee cup before resuming. 'Although I believe that Tudor will be successful in mounting a claim against Mark, I am by no means certain as to how much it might recover. As you all know, Mark received £5 million as his share of the sale proceeds, £1 million of which was in cash and the other £4 million in shares in Tudor, which could not be sold for one year. I understand, however,' here looking to Jeremy for confirmation, 'that the cash element has largely been dissipated, partly in repayment of bank debts, and that there are further bank loans which are secured on the shares in Tudor. So,' here Paul showed some hesitation, 'perhaps the most that Tudor might expect to be able to recover from Mark would be whatever the shares might realise in one year's time, less the amount due to the bank.'

Paul paused for a moment and this time, when he resumed, his voice took on a more measured tone. 'You will by now have realised why it is that I have left the position of Stephens Foster until the end. From Tudor's perspective, Stephens Foster is easily the most attractive target. And if Tudor is to recover its loss, it is an essential and necessary target. It is unlikely that it will be able to recover much more than £2 million from Mark Palmer, particularly when the legal costs of both parties have been met. Which means, even assuming a modest contribution from its own auditors, that Tudor will still be some £7 million short of the sum which it is claiming. That can only come from Stephens Foster.

'Obviously Tudor's lawyers will be aware of your obligatory professional indemnity policy. What they will not yet realise is that the policy has a limit of £3 million.'

Jeremy was crestfallen as he and his partners were reminded of the frightening extent of their under-insurance. Paul's words took on a progressively more serious note as he finally spelt out the brutal implications. 'That would mean that, allowing for both parties' legal expenses, Tudor could seek to recover as much as £5 million from the eight partners of Stephens Foster.' Paul moved quickly to fill the doom-laden void which followed his last sentence.

'Of course, we have not yet considered formally the merits of Tudor's case against Stephens Foster but, as I know that you all realise, it does not hold out very much hope for your firm and its partners. The financial accounts of Palmer, as audited by Stephens Foster, were crucial to the acquisition and to establishing its value. We now know that those accounts were fraudulent. The question to be answered is whether Stephens Foster should have detected the fraud.'

Paul explained (although this was not new to his audience of professional accountants whose main business was auditing) that the courts had established that an auditor could not be expected to detect a complicated and sophisticated fraud. In a now ancient but still celebrated judgement, it had been held that an auditor is a watchdog, not a bloodhound.

'However,' Paul sombrely continued, 'on the basis of the forensic evidence contained in the investigating accountants' report, it would be a very lenient judge who would not feel that the auditors should have uncovered the simplistic falsification carried out by Nigel Kendal.'

Jeremy visibly wilted under this candid but devastating indictment. Paul then sought to end his presentation on a slightly more positive note. 'Although I have given you my own personal and professional judgement, there are a number of contentious areas, including some, as I have already indicated, which have not been fully tested in the courts – such as duty of care. What I now strongly recommend is that we arrange a conference with the leading counsel who will represent you if the case goes to court and get his opinion on the advice and understanding of the law which I have given to you.'

Paul was instructed to arrange for such a meeting at the earliest possible moment and the partners then wearily dispersed to try to resume the normal business of the practice and its clients' affairs.

Jeremy retired to his own room and sat alone. He had never before felt so wretched. He knew that his firm had no defence against a charge of negligence. They had placed too much trust in Nigel Kendal, had been insufficiently vigilant and had been hoodwinked. He felt embarrassed and ashamed. The reputation of Stephens Foster, which he had nurtured and guarded over so many years, would be in ruins and he had let down his client.

But the catastrophic financial consequences seemed out of all proportion. Not only had he failed his client, but also his partners and his family. He had not at first realised – and perhaps he should have – that a fraud which involved the sum of £3 million could escalate into a claim for a loss of £10 million. And if the claim had been for no more than £3 million – even if Stephens Foster were found solely liable, which was unlikely – it would have been covered by the professional indemnity policy. It was the decision to limit the cover under the policy which was responsible for the scale of the calamity.

And it had been *his* decision. He had been obsessed with the rate of increase in premiums, had persuaded his partners that they should not pay the further increases which a higher level of cover would have required, and had maintained the cover at the minimum level laid down by their professional body. It was an obsession which now seemed to have been stupidly unreasonable and which could have devastating implications. If Paul Davis's worst fears were realised, it would mean that Jeremy and his partners would have to pay £5 million from their own resources. It would mean bankruptcy.

Jeremy was not yet sufficiently depressed not to be able to reflect on the irony of the situation in which he now found himself. He had always been excessively prudent in the management of his own financial affairs and in the advice that he had given to his clients on theirs. He had never borrowed large sums to buy a house beyond his own assessment of his means, despite all the golf club banter and pressure about missed opportunities.

And above all, he had avoided Lloyds. He had never understood how people, who in other respects were intelligent, often highly so, could allow a gang of second-raters, most of whom they would not know, to have the unlimited ability to pledge all of their assets. Everybody had known, he believed, that it was the duds who went to work at Lloyds. However, what had not been realised was that, in addition to being incompetents, so many of the underwriters were also crooks. Greed had been the force that had driven normally sensible people into the arms of Lloyds. And although Jeremy had avoided the vice of greed, he was in danger of being brought down to the level of even the most distressed Lloyds 'name' by his excessive parsimony.

Suddenly, for no particular reason that he could identify, but perhaps as a result of the anguish brought on by these morbid and maudlin reflections, he had a vivid memory of his father and then of their last outing together. To Jeremy's everlasting chagrin, at about the same time as he was developing his relationship with his new father-figure, Bill Foster, and establishing his comfortable home in Godalming, his father had died a lonely death in his single room in the rented house in Rochdale where he had lodged.

Their last adventure together was etched as clearly on Jeremy's mind as if it had happened yesterday. It was in January 1948 and Manchester United were to play Aston Villa in the third round of the FA Cup. The match was to be at Villa Park in Birmingham and Jeremy's dad arrived at his grandmother's Manchester home one day clutching two tickets for the game. 'I'll collect yer on Saturday mornin',' he said. 'We can walk together to t'coach station. They've got a "football special" to tek United supporters there n' back.'

Jeremy was in a fever of excited anticipation for the rest of the week and hardly slept on the Friday night before the game. He had watched United play at Maine Road, where they were temporarily accommodated while Old Trafford's war damage was repaired, but he had never been to an away match before. And this was a cup tie!

It turned out to be a game of roller-coaster emotions with the action surging first one way and then the other, and with sudden and dramatic changes of fortune. After the first minute, United were losing by one goal to nil; at half time they were ahead by five goals to one; with five minutes to go, they were struggling – they were still in the lead but now only by five goals to four; the final score was six–four.

United were destined to go on to win the cup in that year, at a time long before trophy winning had become routine to them and when Manchester City was still the dominant Manchester club. But it was the game at Villa Park which would always remain in Jeremy's memory and he could still, without a moment's hesitation, recall every member of the United team who played in that game, particularly the forward line of Delaney, Morris, Rowley, Pearson and Mitten.

However, the drama on the pitch was almost matched, in Jeremy's memory, by what took place off it. Villa Park had been more than full to capacity. He was later told that the attendance was in excess of 80,000. Within the crowd it was difficult for Jeremy to follow all of the action on the pitch and as half time approached, Jeremy heard a friendly voice in his ear. 'Cum on, kid, let's get yer over the wall.'

And, with his dad's encouragement, the man hoisted Jeremy on to his shoulders and deposited him on the grass at the side of the touch-line, where he settled amongst a growing number of other schoolboys.

That was the last he saw of his dad. When the game was over, he searched, in vain, for any sign of him but, as the ground cleared of spectators, he was nowhere to be seen. Jeremy wandered disconsolately out of the ground towards the coach park and then, almost in despair, through the ranks of hundreds of similar looking coaches with their engines already running. It was dark and cold, and had started to rain. Some of the coaches had left and others were now leaving. Suddenly, by a stroke of enormous good fortune, he saw the distinctive signage of the coach on which he had arrived. It had passed its departure time but was waiting for the missing passengers – Jeremy and his dad. The driver waited a further fifteen minutes and then set off – without Jeremy's dad.

Jeremy completed the journey by walking alone from the bus station back to his grandmother's house. Still no sign of dad. More than three hours later, he eventually turned up, looking the worse for wear. He had gone for a drink at half time and had not found his way back. Jeremy's grandmother was unforgiving. But Jeremy had only fond, happy memories of his last day out with his dad.

Jeremy was disturbed from this deep reverie by his secretary, who delivered the news that a meeting had been arranged with Mr Edward Walsh QC at his chambers in Lincoln's Inn in two days' time.

CHAPTER TWENTY-THREE

Jeremy had arrived for the conference with leading counsel in a state of apprehension. Edward Walsh presided in a large, high-ceilinged, second-floor room overlooking the greenery and now sparsely leafed trees of Lincoln's Inn Fields. He sat behind a large old-fashioned desk, which was littered with papers and law books and be-ribboned briefs, most of which were not relevant to the case which he had just begun to discuss. There were a number of ancient leather armchairs scattered around the room, which were occupied by Jeremy and his junior partner, and Paul Davis from Fisons, Stephens Foster's solicitors, and his assistant, while another barrister from Edward Walsh's chambers – who would be his junior if the case were to go to court – was perched on the windowsill.

Edward Walsh, a tall, elegant figure in an impeccably cut Savile Row suit, contrasted sharply with the shabby gentility of his surroundings. He had a large head and a warm, open and friendly face with a florid, rhubarb-and-cream complexion. He was not at all the austere figure whom Jeremy had imagined from his reputation as one of the country's leading Chancery 'silks'. He spoke in a low, soft voice, with what Jeremy thought might be a faint Irish brogue. Jeremy had to concentrate hard to catch all of his words.

Mr Walsh said that he had studied the formal advice which had been prepared by Paul Davis and was in broad agreement with his conclusions and with his interpretation of the law. He said that he did not believe that it would be a constructive use of the time which they had together if he were simply to comment on all of the issues raised by Paul. That could be covered in his written opinion. What he did want to do, he said, was to raise a new issue that did not appear to have been considered.

'What,' said Mr Walsh, 'was the value of the consideration with which Tudor acquired Palmer?' Jeremy looked puzzled and did not immediately respond. However, as it became clear that the eminent barrister was awaiting a reply, Jeremy answered, a little hesitantly.

'But, of course, as we all know, the purchase consideration was £15 million.'

'Ah,' said Mr Walsh, 'but it was not. It was 7½ million new ordinary shares in Tudor. And how do we know what *they* were worth?'

An increasingly confused Jeremy attempted to answer this further, what he thought pointless, question. 'Each Tudor share was valued on the stock market at the time of the acquisition at £2 and, therefore, the issue of 7½ million shares provided the £15 million consideration.'

'If I understand these matters correctly,' said Mr Walsh, 'the value of Tudor's shares on the stock market would have been influenced by the published financial statements issued by Tudor. What if those statements could be shown to be incorrect? Let me explain further. The Palmer business was originally valued at £15 million. That was based on the profit figures shown in Palmer's accounts. Subsequently, those profit figures were reduced as a result of the reversal of the fraudulent entries. The new value based on the new profit figures, or so Tudor would have us believe, is now only £5 million, a reduction of £10 million.

'Well, what is sauce for the goose can also be sauce for the gander. Mr Mason,' and here he waved in the direction of his still precariously perched junior, 'has been looking through the press cuttings on Tudor, and there have been a number of questions raised about its accounting policies. It has been suggested that the reported profits might have been flattered and that more prudent policies would reduce those profits. Let us assume – and it is, I agree, a very large assumption – that we could demonstrate to the satisfaction of the courts that Tudor's profits were overstated. Then we could argue that the share price had been inflated and that the true value of the shares issued for the acquisition of Palmer – the purchase consideration – was not £15 million but a lower figure. And that would have a corresponding effect on Tudor's so-called loss.'

Jeremy was bewildered by what he saw as Mr Walsh's naïve line of enquiry and he suddenly blurted out. 'But how on earth could we possibly do that? The top financial analysts in the City and some of the best brains at the *Financial Times* and other newspapers have examined every aspect of Tudor's affairs and, although questions have been raised, nothing has been found which could be made to stick.'

Mr Walsh smiled broadly as he replied. 'They did not have the weapons which we now have. As Paul Davis well understands, there is, in litigation, a process called discovery. Stephens Foster, as defendant, is entitled to ask, through its solicitors, for copies of any documents held by the plaintiff, Tudor, which would be important for its defence. The courts would need to be satisfied that the documents requested were relevant to the action, but I believe that it should be possible to prepare an argument that, in the circumstances of this particular case, for Stephens Foster to mount a proper defence, it will need to see copies of all of the documents and files, including correspondence with its auditors, which support Tudor's published financial statements. We would need to make it clear to the court, and to Tudor, that we plan to attack the value which has been attributed to the purchase consideration and that we will, therefore, be questioning the accounting policies and practices pursued by Tudor. And it is for this reason, we will argue, that we will need to see copies of the support documentation for Tudor's accounts. They could make very interesting reading and, if it gets to court,' Mr Walsh stated with some animation, 'they will provide useful ammunition to be used in cross-examining Gerald Howard under oath.

'At the very least, it will make the other side realise that we are not entirely without resource and that we aim to counterattack rather than simply to lie down and die.'

Jeremy felt as if the most enormous weight had been lifted from his shoulders. He felt better than at any time since that ill-fated day on the third Thursday in September. He was inspired by the possibility of a counterattack and almost ecstatic at the prospect of Gerald Howard being cross-examined in the witness box by Mr Walsh. He could hardly wait to hear of the reaction from Tudor's arrogant, cocky City lawyers when they received Paul Davis's letter on discovery with its long, long list of requested files and documents. But, most important of all, there suddenly seemed to be hope.

CHAPTER TWENTY-FOUR

Gerald Howard was also experiencing a mood swing. His anger and outrage at what he had convinced himself were Mark Palmer's calculated fraudulent actions had slowly been replaced by the pleasure and satisfaction which he was now feeling at the prospect of bringing about Mark's total humiliation and ruin. Tudor's own lawyers, Faber and Freeman, the sharp venomous City firm whom Jeremy had found so unpalatable, had given advice that was remarkably similar to that received by Stephens Foster from Paul Davis.

'Stephens Foster,' Faber and Freeman had written, 'with their professional indemnity insurers standing behind them, offer a relatively easy target. They have clearly been negligent and the existence of the insurance policy means that they will have the necessary resources to meet the claim.' Although Fisons had, in the usual manner, refused to disclose any information with regard to the existence of insurance cover, Faber and Freeman knew that Stephens Foster would have been obliged to have such cover by their professional body.

Negotiations with Tudor's own auditors had already started and were progressing well. The friendly and co-operative nature of the discussions had led Gerald to believe that an acceptable settlement could be reached without the need for litigation. It would make only a small contribution to the total amount of the loss but, at the very least, it would cover the legal costs of pursuing the more substantive claims against Stephens Foster and Mark Palmer.

It was the thought of pounding Mark Palmer into the ground that had Gerald almost salivating. Faber and Freeman had suggested to Gerald that a possible approach might be to seek a settlement with Mark which, while extracting a large sum of money from him, would still leave him with something left over. This would have the attraction of offering an incentive to Mark to reach a quick resolution, for if it went to court he would run the risk of finishing up with nothing at all. It would save on legal costs, the bill for which would eventually be picked up by Tudor if Mark had by then lost everything, and the balance of the claim, Tudor's advisers assumed, could, in any event, be recovered from Stephens Foster.

Gerald had rejected this suggestion out of hand. He was determined to squeeze every last penny out of Mark Palmer and to make him realise that he had made the worst mistake of his life by crossing Gerald Howard. And the prospect of a possibly long-drawn-out legal process from which most people would have recoiled was something that Gerald now positively relished. He was going to savour – preferably slowly – the downfall of Mark Palmer.

Tudor had issued a low-key statement to the stock market to the effect that certain discrepancies had been found in the financial affairs of Palmer subsequent to the acquisition and that steps were being taken to secure compensation. Shareholders were told that it would not affect the trading performance or financial position of Tudor and that the board was confident that any loss would be recovered. Gerald had to balance the legal requirement to make an announcement against the need not to cause any undue alarm. The twin messages being, 'there is no real problem' and 'everything is under control'.

And Gerald believed that to be a fair assessment of the situation. He had the clearest advice that he should be successful in recovering virtually the whole of the £10 million claim, with Stephens Foster and their insurers being the banker, and Mark Palmer providing the light relief. The cash injection from the claims would more than compensate for Palmer's profit shortfall and it would provide Anthony Kemp and his team of accountants with further opportunities for enhancing earnings. It now seemed likely that the City's best expectations for Tudor's profits would be met and the thought of the risk of a profits warning was no more than a distant memory. Gerald had every reason to feel satisfied with life.

When Faber and Freeman received the first letter from Fisons, with its request for extensive and detailed financial information and for reams of documents relating to Tudor's accounts and financial affairs, their reaction was surprisingly relaxed. Paul Davis's letter had run to several pages but Tudor's solicitor's reply was short and to the point: 'Tudor has no intention of supplying any of the information requested and we would remind you that it is your clients who are being sued for their gross and irresponsible negligence. You would be better engaged in advising your clients to face up to the consequences of the inevitable settlement at the earliest possible moment.'

Anthony Kemp was routinely sent a copy of the exchange of correspondence. When he read Paul Davis's long letter, his response was a little less cool. He immediately rang Faber and Freeman in a state of some agitation to make it clear that if Tudor had to supply only a fraction of the information requested, it could be extremely damaging to its reputation. His lawyers sought to calm his fears: 'Fisons' letter bears all the hallmarks of a desperate last-ditch effort of a tawdry defence to muddy the waters. It is a scatter-gun approach which Fisons might hope will yield a few titbits of embarrassing material but which,' they concluded, 'no judge will allow.'

Fisons' next missive to Faber and Freeman was to say that, after the benefit of counsel's advice, they were to take the matter of disclosure before the courts as soon as was convenient. Faber and Freeman would be informed of the date of the hearing. Anthony Kemp was again sent a copy of the letter and his solicitors had again sought to reassure him that he had no cause for concern: 'It is a mischief-making diversionary tactic, which is,' they wrote, 'doomed to failure.' Nonetheless, leading counsel was to be instructed to appear for Tudor at the hearing.

*

Before the issue of discovery could be brought formally before a judge for his ruling, there was a preliminary skirmish as Faber and Freeman, alerted by a now increasingly anxious Anthony Kemp, expressed concern about an issue of such a sensitive nature being aired in open court. Counsel for Tudor, on instructions from Faber and Freeman, argued that it could be harmful to Tudor's reputation.

The judge had accepted this argument and had agreed to hear the submissions in the privacy of his chambers. Three days later, therefore, counsel for Tudor and for Stephens Foster gathered before Mr Justice Templewood at the Law Courts in the Strand. Edward Walsh QC, together with his junior, Charles Mason, appeared for Stephens Foster, and Victor Showman, QC, a barrister of similar lustre to Mr Walsh, and who was also accompanied by a junior, led for Tudor. Mr Justice Templewood had a reputation as a stickler for discipline and procedure when presiding in his court, but in the seclusion of his chambers he preferred a more relaxed and informal regime. He and the two leading counsel were on easy and familiar terms with each other and the judge asked, in a friendly way, if Mr Walsh would outline his complaint. Mr Walsh explained that Stephens Foster was preparing its defence against an action for damages brought by Tudor Holdings, for whom Mr Showman was appearing.

'I appear for Stephens Foster, a long established and reputable firm of professional accountants,' said Mr Walsh. 'It is being alleged that they were negligent in auditing the accounts of their client company, Palmer Industries Ltd. Palmer was subsequently acquired by Tudor and Tudor is now seeking to recover, by way of damages, the loss which it alleges it has incurred as a direct result of the alleged negligence.

'Judge, the allegations levelled against us are of the gravest kind. If they were upheld, the damage to the professional reputation of Stephens Foster would be incalculable. And the amount claimed by way of compensation is of such a size as, should it be granted, would bring about the financial ruin of the firm and of its partners. So, the issues are of the most serious nature and we are quite properly concerned to prepare a full and detailed defence.

'To enable us to prepare that defence, we have requested through solicitors, certain financial information and documents under the process of discovery. The list of the requested material and the exchange of correspondence has been handed to your lordship. We believe that this information is relevant to the case and that it is vital for the proper preparation of our defence. As you will see, Tudor has refused to comply. We have approached your lordship for a ruling on the matter.'

Mr Justice Templewood looked quizzically towards Victor Showman. 'And how do you reply to that, Mr Showman?' Mr Showman bobbed his head slightly towards Mr Justice Templewood in an almost absent-minded recognition of the semi-formality of the occasion, 'My lordship, I can afford to be brief, as the proposal is entirely without merit, and, I am tempted to say, vexatious. Tudor Holdings is a large successful company, publicly quoted on the Stock Exchange. To attempt to supply the enormous quantity of detailed information that has been requested would place an intolerable burden on its most senior management and would deflect them from the proper running of its business. However, that is not the main argument against this desperate application. The case, in connection with which this application has been made, is based on the simple issue of negligence. As my learned friend has very helpfully explained to your lordship, we will be arguing that Stephens Foster was negligent in auditing the accounts of Palmer Industries. That is all that this case is about: the negligence of Stephens Foster. That being the situation, how on earth can a host of detailed financial information relating to the affairs of Tudor Holdings be relevant to the issue of Stephens Foster's negligent audit?

'My lordship,' he concluded, 'this application is not relevant to the issues raised in this litigation. The information requested is not necessary for Stephens Foster's proper defence and, in our view, it is a frivolous application bordering on harassment, which abuses the process of discovery.'

Mr Justice Templewood turned towards Edward Walsh. 'Mr Showman seems to have a point, Mr Walsh,' he said, silkily, 'how is this application relevant to the charge of negligence?'

Edward Walsh now played his trump card: 'But negligence is *not* the only issue in this litigation,' he said with emphasis, as he again rose to his feet. 'There is also the question of damages. If the court finds for the plaintiff on the issue of negligence, then, as I explained in my opening, there is a claim for compensation for the loss which it is alleged has been incurred as a result of that negligence. The calculation of that alleged loss is based on the original purchase consideration for Palmer Industries compared to a new ascribed value now given to Palmer based on its reduced profits. The price paid for Palmer – the consideration – consisted entirely of ordinary shares in Tudor. We will be arguing in our defence,' and here, Mr Walsh spoke with even greater emphasis, 'that Tudor's profits have been inflated by the use of dubious accounting policies. We will argue that if the true profits had been declared, then the share price would have been lower and the purchase consideration received by the vendors of Palmer, based on that share price, would also have been lower. Any claim for compensation for its alleged loss would, therefore, be reduced and might, in fact, be eliminated.

'The attack on Tudor's published profit figures,' said Mr Walsh, now in full flow, 'will form a major part of our defence and, if that defence is to be properly prepared, it is essential that we receive the information requested with regard to the background to Tudor's accounting policies and financial affairs.'

Mr Walsh sat down with an obvious show of satisfaction and with an expression on his face that an unkind person might have thought to be a smirk. Mr Justice Templewood's friendly demeanour had hardened a little. 'That puts an entirely different complexion on matters and,' here, he directed a gentle reprimand towards Mr Walsh, 'it might have been more helpful if the whole of your arguments had been presented at the outset.'

If Mr Justice Templewood had been slightly discomposed by Mr Walsh's concluding statement, it was as nothing to the disarray to which Mr Showman had now been reduced. When asked for his reaction to Mr Walsh's latest argument, there was a suggestion of panic and bluster. 'It would be unprecedented to allow the dissection of the accounts of a publicly quoted company in open court in a case of this nature. There is no justification for the wild and outrageous statement with regard to Tudor's published profits but,' he complained, 'mud inevitably sticks and, if the defence is to be given the opportunity to repeat those statements publicly, it would be seriously damaging to Tudor's interests as well as being contrary to public policy. It would be wrong,' he argued, 'to allow the discovery process to be used as some form of fishing expedition to bolster a disgraceful and irresponsible defence.'

'Unprecedented' was a word that featured several times in Mr Showman's less than usually eloquent response. It was a word that Mr Justice Templewood picked up on when he brought the proceedings to an end. 'I will look at any relevant precedents and will deliver my reply to the application in writing during the course of the next two days.'

CHAPTER TWENTY-FIVE

Within an hour of the delivery of Mr Justice Templewood's ruling, a crisis meeting was being held in Gerald Howard's Knightsbridge office. The ruling had been in favour of Stephens Foster and Tudor had been instructed to provide copies of the documents and to supply the information that had been requested by Fisons in its long, three-page list. Tudor had been given fourteen days in which to comply.

Gerald had only recently become aware of the discovery process. He had assumed, had been advised, that the issues in the lawsuit were clear-cut and, apart from ensuring that the maximum amount of humiliation was heaped upon Mark Palmer, he had left the detailed work to Anthony Kemp and the lawyers. When the question of discovery had been taken before a judge for a ruling, Anthony had thought it prudent to alert Gerald, but he had played down its importance, suggesting that it was little more than a routine try-on with a pre-determined outcome. The news this morning, therefore, had, for Gerald, been a totally unexpected bombshell. He had immediately convened an emergency meeting, which started as soon as the Faber and Freeman partner had scrambled out of his taxi into the lift and into Gerald's office. Anthony completed the trio.

Gerald was, for the first time, looking at copies of the exchange of letters between Fisons and Faber and Freeman. There were intermittent explosions as his eye caught each new impertinent request. 'Copies of all the supporting schedules for each of the items in the published accounts. Copies of all internal memoranda with regard to the preparation of the accounts and with regard to accounting policies. Copies of correspondence with the auditors . . . ' he broke off and almost shouted at the newly chastened lawyer. 'And all within fourteen days! That is impossible!

'We would need to examine with great care all of the documents and letters and it would take weeks of work from our most senior people. It would then need a seven-ton pantechnicon to deliver it. It cannot be done,' he said with finality. The lawyer was looking more and more uncomfortable. The bounce and bombast had disappeared.

'But Gerald,' he said, 'we have no option. We must abide by the judge's ruling otherwise you will be in contempt of court. And,' he continued, a trifle prissily, 'it is important that you are not selective in the information which you provide. You must supply every document in the relevant files. As an officer of the court,' he concluded, weakly, 'I have a responsibility to make sure that you comply and that you do not extract any papers which you feel might be embarrassing.'

Gerald looked at him in horror but then he quickly changed tack. 'Tell me, assuming that we provide all this garbage, what will they do with it?'

The reply was measured, with each word chosen carefully. 'Fisons have now made it perfectly clear that they plan to attack Tudor's profit record. They then hope to undermine the basis for the share price which was used in financing the Palmer deal. When Fisons receive all the documents and other material, they will sift through them, probably with the help of accountants, to identify any which they can use to cast doubt on the profit figures. They will then use the documents that they believe will be helpful to their cause in court, as part of their defence. They will have an expert witness, again almost certainly an accountant, to interpret the documents for the benefit of the court and to explain their relevance to the calculation of Tudor's profits.' Almost as an afterthought, he then added, 'And of course, Gerald, when you are required to give your own evidence in court, it is quite likely that the defence will wish to cross-examine you on this issue.'

Gerald had heard enough. He brusquely informed the Faber and Freeman partner that he and Anthony now wished to discuss the matter together and the dejected lawyer was only too pleased to leave the room. As soon as they were alone together, Gerald's pent-up fury was unleashed. Inevitably, it was directed at Anthony. 'This whole fucking, stupid, unbelievable situation is entirely your responsibility. *You* appointed the auditors to investigate Palmer. *You* supervised their work and *you* failed to detect the simplest, most fucking straightforward fraud in the book,' he raged. But this time Anthony was prepared for the outburst. Partly in a fit of pique, but more calculatedly as a pre-emptive move in anticipation of Gerald's venom, he had, that morning, dismissed the head office accountant who had been most directly involved with the auditors in the Palmer investigation. He had not yet told Gerald of this move as he did not, unless and until it became absolutely necessary, want to be seen to be accepting any kind of direct responsibility for the débâcle.

Now Anthony remained calm and waited silently for Gerald's anger to subside. He then spoke quietly, but firmly. 'Gerald, we have to find a way out of this. If we continue, we will be destroyed. We both know what a tame accountant acting as an expert witness for the other side can make of our profit figures. And, if you are cross-examined on our accounts in the witness box, you will be crucified. We must seek a solution. And that needs to happen sooner, rather than later; before they realise quite what a strong hand they hold.'

Gerald's filthy temper had not entirely dissipated. 'So what do you suggest we do?' he spat out.

Anthony maintained his air of calm determination. 'Gerald, we must settle. We will negotiate the best deal that is available but we must settle. And we must settle quickly.'

Gerald looked through his office windows towards Hyde Park, apparently lost in thought, and did not respond for several minutes. He had felt a rising tide of nausea and panic as Tudor's lawyer had spelt out the implications of the discovery process. Events were running out of control. He no longer had an appetite for this particular fight and he wanted to bring it to an end. 'Settle,' he eventually replied, with a tired air of resignation. 'And Anthony,' a deflated Gerald concluded wearily, 'you handle it but keep me closely in touch. I will want an update from you each morning.'

Anthony Kemp relished the opportunity of rescuing, without the dominating presence of Gerald Howard, whatever consolation prizes might still be recovered from the wreckage of their legal actions. Anthony did not have quite the same emotional capital invested in the litigation as Gerald and was, therefore, now able to take a more dispassionate view. Nonetheless, he was fully aware of the very serious nature of this setback to Tudor's fortunes and of the impact that it would have on its prospects.

It was a major reverse. They had had every reason to believe that they would have been successful in recovering the very generous calculation of Tudor's supposed loss on the Palmer acquisition. And if they had not quite already spent the expected proceeds, the prospective £10 million of compensation payments had certainly featured in Tudor's future financial planning and were an important and essential element in its ability to meet the stock market's profit expectations. In the end they had been outmanoeuvred. The proposal to use the discovery process as a means of attacking Tudor's profit record had proved to be fatal. The irony was that the other side could not possibly have realised quite how potent that line of attack would prove to be. And Anthony's first priority was to make absolutely certain that they did not find out.

He needed to show urgency without suggesting panic. It was explained through lawyers that compliance with the discovery judgement would impose an intolerable burden on Tudor's most senior management, which was consistent with the earlier pleadings. A further elaboration was that Tudor was currently involved in a new, major project that demanded the attention of those same managers. An early settlement might therefore be possible, it was said, on terms which would be more advantageous to Fisons' client, if it could be speedily resolved and so avoid the burden of the discovery process.

It was made clear that if a satisfactory agreement could not be reached then, regardless of the inconvenience, Tudor would comply with the judgement. Fevered discussions took place between solicitors to seek to establish just how advantageous the new terms might be. When Stephens Foster's insurers heard that the settlement might actually be below the £3 million value of their cover – a figure which they had already mentally written off – and that it would also mean an end to the rapidly escalating legal costs, agreement was quickly reached. Stephens Foster (in fact, their insurers) were to pay £2 million in cash to Tudor in full and final settlement but without any admission of liability, and each party was to bear its own costs. There was a tight confidentiality clause, which prevented any of the parties from disclosing any details of the settlement, other than those required by Stock Exchange regulations.

As soon as the Stephens Foster litigation was finalised, Anthony sought to settle the Mark Palmer case. He was obviously aware of Gerald's strong and, he thought, irrational feelings with regard to Mark but Anthony was determined to conclude the matter quickly before Mark's lawyers became aware of the all-too-successful ploy which had been used by Stephens Foster. After some preliminary jousting, the lawsuit had easily been resolved by the payment of £750,000 by a no doubt much relieved Mark Palmer.

Together with a contribution from Tudor's auditors – that particular issue had been settled as expected, in an amicable manner – the total amount received by Tudor amounted to £3 million. Anthony had made the best of a difficult job because, if his bluff had been called, he could not possibly have allowed the case to go to court. But it was a long, long way short of the £10 million figure that Tudor had confidently anticipated. The compensation payment would still allow Anthony a modest opportunity to massage the soon-to-be-announced profit figures. But the very best that Anthony could now hope for was that he could cobble together figures which might just reach the minimum expectations of the most pessimistic of the analysts. It would be touch and go.

A bald announcement was made to the Stock Exchange to the effect that Tudor had received the sum of £3 million in settlement of the claims arising from the Palmer acquisition's accounting discrepancies.

CHAPTER TWENTY-SIX

Each year the cricket association to which Tom Curtis's team belonged held a dinner at one of the large Park Lane hotels. There would usually be a celebrity speaker – this year it was to be Christopher Martin-Jenkins, the chief cricket correspondent for *The Times* – and cups and prizes were awarded to the league and knock-out competition winners, as well as for the best performances with bat and ball.

This year Tom was to receive the trophy for the best bowling figures – he had taken seven wickets for only fourteen runs, in a game which his team had still managed to lose – and he and Rebecca disembarked from their taxi at the hotel on a wet Saturday evening towards the end of November. They could not entirely avoid the rain as, due to a congestion of taxis, they had to walk the final few yards – Rebecca in her high heels – to the hotel entrance. The dinner had a reputation for being a boozy affair and it was clear that not many of those attending were planning to drive themselves home.

The food was a bland and tasteless product of mass-market catering but the wine, if not of the highest quality, was plentiful. Christopher Martin-Jenkins made a witty, not-too-long speech and, in presenting Tom with his award, he referred to his employment with a rival broadsheet newspaper. The wine during dinner was included in the ticket price, which was usually a formula to guarantee over-indulgence but despite this, or perhaps because of it, there was a general drift to the cash bar after the speeches. Tom and Rebecca joined in the crush together with another couple from their table and, to celebrate the occasion and his prize, and in an excess of gregariousness brought on by the wine, he ordered a bottle of champagne.

As the champagne was nearing its end, Tom was approached by a figure who seemed vaguely familiar and who had been standing by the bar for several minutes, waiting, it seemed, for an opportunity to introduce himself. As soon as he caught Tom's attention, Tom recognised him as a member of a rival cricket team. He reminded Tom that his name was Julian Greene and went on to say that, although he realised that this was the most inopportune time, he wished to speak to Tom on a matter which was both urgent and confidential. Tom moved slightly away from his party and asked what it was about. Although both had obviously drunk a fair amount of alcohol, they had been affected differently. Tom had developed an amiable, hail-fellow-well-met mood, while Julian seemed agitated and excitable.

The reason for this agitation soon became clear. 'Until I heard Christopher Martin-Jenkins tonight,' he said to Tom, 'I had not realised that you were the Tom Curtis who wrote for the *Financial Times*. I have a big story for you. I know that you write from time to time about Tudor Holdings, and I am an accountant,' Julian explained, 'who, until a week ago, worked in the head office finance department at Tudor. There is a major scandal about the acquisition of Palmer and I have the facts and the documents to prove it.'

Whistleblowers are notoriously unpopular and Tom was always wary of vengeful and bitter sacked executives who tried to do down their former employers. But the mention of Tudor whetted his appetite. He had seen the two anodyne press releases about the accounting discrepancies at Palmer and he was curious to know what lay behind them. It was agreed that Julian would telephone Tom at his office on Monday morning and they could then discuss the matter further.

Having apparently unburdened himself, Julian became more relaxed. Tom ordered another bottle of champagne and Julian and Tom were quickly new best friends. The conversation moved to cricket and then to football. Julian played every Sunday morning in a pick-up game of football in Hyde Park. He urged Tom to join him the following morning. Tom had not played football since his schooldays and treasured his Sunday mornings at home with Rebecca. But Julian was insistent. The issue was settled when Julian said that he would bring along the Tudor papers and that they would then be able to discuss them over a pint of beer after the game rather than wait until Monday morning. Partly as a result of the influence of the champagne, but also from a desire not to allow Julian too much time for reflection, and perhaps second thoughts, on Tudor, Tom agreed to go along. They arranged to meet in Hyde Park at eleven o'clock.

The following morning, Tom left Rebecca's warm bed with great reluctance. In the cold light of day it seemed a stupid thing to be doing. Rebecca thought that he was mad but, knowing that it had some connection with Tudor, and honouring their pact not to discuss Tudor's affairs together, she raised little objection. He drove from Parsons Green to Hyde Park and, struggling to focus his tired eyes into the still-drizzling rain, it occurred to him, rather belatedly, that his alcohol level might still be above the legal limit after the previous night's over-indulgence. However, there was little he could do about that now, he thought, as he nevertheless prudently modified his speed.

He silently repeated to himself Julian's directions – north end of the park, by the Bayswater Road, opposite Albion Street, and under a large oak tree. He was soon parking the car by the side of the road and walking towards a small group of similarly attired men, who were sheltering from the rain under the protection of the oak tree. Tom did not possess a pair of football boots but Julian had suggested that training shoes would be all right, and Tom had rooted out an old pair of trainers and some tracksuit bottoms, which he had kept at Rebecca's flat. Trudging apprehensively through the mixture of sodden grass and treacherous-looking mud, he could well imagine the value of proper studded football boots and envisaged spending half the morning on his backside.

Julian had already arrived and introduced Tom to several of his new team-mates. They were a strange mixture and of many nationalities, including three Italian waiters, an Egyptian whose name was Ahmed, a large Hungarian named Stefan (who turned out to be the chef at the Arts Club), an American student, an actor from the Royal Shakespeare Company, a hairdresser and three more typical Londoners who worked in the City. The tradition of this Sunday morning football match, Tom was told, had been established for many years, but nobody was able to say quite when or how it had started. People became aware of it by word of mouth and new members came along as others dropped out. The core group, however, were the City slickers (as they seemed to Tom) and Julian. They rarely missed a match and one of their number had been known to return early from overseas business trips so as to make the Sunday morning game.

The two teams were chosen and there were eight on each side. Tom soon realised that he was not quite as fit as he had thought. Most of the players were much younger than him, some of the Italians seemed still to be in their teens and one or two of them were very good. And they all took it so seriously. After each short, sharp burst of energy, chasing a long ball or pursuing an opponent, Tom was left panting, out of breath, with his hands on his knees. It was a far cry from his more gentle sport of cricket, where he could trundle slowly up to the wicket to bowl his off-spinners.

At half past twelve when the game ended – Tom's team had won – he was more than ready for the promised pint. About half of the group, Tom limping with a bruised ankle, the legacy of a crushing tackle from Stefan, crossed the Bayswater Road and walked into Hyde Park Gardens to find the pub. This was also part of the tradition.

Tom and Julian took their beers to a side table, while the rest of the, now noisy, group stayed at the bar. They were soon discussing the subject that had enticed Tom away from his usual, and much looked-forward-to, lazy Sunday morning with Rebecca. 'The acquisition of Palmer is a disaster,' said Julian, 'and the so-called accounting discrepancies are nothing less than blatant fraud. A business which Tudor bought for £15 million is now valued at only £5 million,' he exclaimed with such emphasis that he lost much of his beer as it slurped from his glass.

He took Tom through the details of the defence's plan to expose Tudor's accounting policies and practices in open court, an exposure which, he said, would have been catastrophic for Tudor. This, said Julian, was why Tudor had settled for £3 million, rather than the £10 million loss that it claimed it had incurred. Julian said that he had been intimately involved in the whole process, working for Tudor until he had been fired in a spiteful act of self-defence by Anthony Kemp. And this to Tom was clearly Julian's revenge. He had brought documentary support for his contentions, including a copy of the judgement on discovery by Mr Justice Templewood.

But it was the specific examples of the way in which Tudor had inflated its profits that really excited Tom. Costs that should properly have been charged against revenue – which would have reduced profits – had been capitalised and carried forward in the balance sheet. And profits had been increased further by bringing forward revenues – such as turnover-related rebates from suppliers – which properly belonged to future accounting periods. It was the sheer scale of these figures that Tom found so shocking. Julian was able to show Tom copies of correspondence with the auditors, which demonstrated that, after some half-hearted questioning, they had agreed to sign off the accounts that included these more than dubious transactions. Tom's pulses were again racing, but this time it was not the fruitless pursuit of a football that was responsible. This really did seem to be a story. Tom took the copies of the documents with him and said that he would speak to Julian at his home the following morning. He then drove back to join Rebecca for a late Sunday brunch.

CHAPTER TWENTY-SEVEN

Tom fidgeted impatiently as he sat at the *Financial Times* Monday morning editorial conference. He was there to represent the Company News pages but first he had to listen to a discussion of the major national and international news stories. The continuing financial meltdown in Japan was the main item but, after the inevitable temperature-taking on the issue of the Euro and some consideration of the slow-down in UK retail sales, it was Tom's turn. He straightaway raised the Tudor affair.

'This story,' he said, 'involves a cover-up. Tudor has incurred a loss, which it has calculated at £10 million, on a business that it had acquired for £15 million, only months earlier. But shareholders have not been informed. All that shareholders have been told is that a sum of £3 million has been recovered in respect of accounting discrepancies. What shareholders have *not* been told is that this is in satisfaction of a claim for £10 million, which had seemed to be well founded but which has now been abandoned.

'That is the cover-up. But the main story is the reason for that cover-up. The key plank in the defence to the claim for £10 million was to have been an attack on Tudor's accounting policies and profit record. And Tudor was so alarmed at the consequences of such an attack, and at what might be revealed in court, that they effectively gave away almost £7 million of shareholders' money. What does Tudor have to hide? That is the real story.'

All those in the editor's room knew the consequences of making unsubstantiated allegations of the kind that Tom was now suggesting and he was anxious to point to the substantial documentary backing that he already had for his story, including the crucial correspondence with the Tudor auditors. Nonetheless, he was told that much work still needed to be done to satisfy both the editor and the newspaper's lawyers before the story could run.

When Tom got back to his desk, his first call was to Julian Greene. He tried to persuade Julian to agree to sign a written statement that would confirm all that he had said. But Julian was beginning to get cold feet. Although, in the rush to dispose of his services, he had not been required by Tudor to sign a formal confidentiality agreement, he knew that he had breached the normally understood legal requirements for confidentiality in the position that he had held. He told Tom that he was not prepared to add anything to what he had said and that he had already said too much. He was insistent that his name must not be used in any article. Tom was thankful that he had sacrificed his Sunday morning for the football match in Hyde Park. His faint premonition that Julian's nerve might not hold had been accurate, but at least he had the copies of the documents that Julian had provided and his note of their meeting.

Tom now settled down to make a series of further telephone calls from the list that he had already prepared. He began with Gerald Howard but, having told Gerald's secretary the nature of the enquiry, he was put through to Anthony Kemp. Anthony was brief and very much to the point. 'I have absolutely nothing to add to the statements which have already been made to the Stock Exchange on the matter of the accounting discrepancies at Palmer,' he said. 'I refuse to take any further questions,' at which point he put down the telephone. Within minutes, Tudor's suave public relations consultant, Rebecca's boss, Giles Sutton, was on the phone to Tom to say that all the relevant facts on Palmer had been disclosed, that there was no story and that – this, with a hint of menace in his voice – they would look very carefully at anything that might be published.

Tom then rang, in quick succession, Tudor's auditors, Palmer's auditors, Tudor's solicitors, Palmer's solicitors and (this last name having been given to Tom by Julian Greene), the partner at the firm of accountants who had carried out the independent investigation.

All were tight-lipped. Nobody was prepared to say anything at all, either on or off the record. Tom then tried Mark Palmer's home number and Mark picked up the phone. He was a little less guarded and less professional than the others. He conceded that he had been required to sign a tough confidentiality agreement, and Tom knew that, in itself, that was not surprising. What did surprise Tom was how chipper Mark seemed. For somebody who had lost his job and his business, and who must have made a substantial contribution to the settlement, Tom found it quite extraordinary. He concluded that however dire the outcome had been for Mark, he must have feared that it could have been even worse.

Tom's final call was to Nigel Kendal. Nigel had certainly not been a party to any confidentiality agreement. He had been summarily dismissed, without compensation and without references. He felt aggrieved. He had convinced himself that he had acted only in the best interests of the company and of Mark Palmer, and that he was now the scapegoat. Since his departure, he had been treated as a pariah by his former colleagues at Tudor and Palmer. He had, however, in the absence of any other worthwhile occupation, continued to take an obsessive interest in Tudor's affairs. He had, from occasional contact with Mark, been aware of the fact that Tudor was seeking £10 million in compensation for the Palmer discrepancies. And Mark's lawyers had apparently confirmed to Mark the strength of Tudor's case. Nigel had, therefore, been astonished to read in his newspaper of the settlement. Feeling that he had little to lose, he conveyed the gist of this to Tom. But when Tom pressed him on the possible reasons for Tudor settling for such a modest figure, he was either not able, or not willing to be of any further help.

Tom reviewed the limited results of his telephone calls. Although he had gathered together some more circumstantial evidence, there were no new hard facts to add to and support the documentary evidence from Julian and Tom's interview notes from his talk with Julian. He discussed the matter with his editor and it was decided that it would not be possible to publish anything in the next day's newspaper, but that they would talk again in the morning.

*

154

After Tom left his desk at the *Financial Times*, he went directly to the TGR bridge club by Marble Arch (just opposite the venue of the previous day's football match), where he had arranged to meet Rebecca. TGR's was a high-stake rubber bridge club named after the late Irving Rose, 'The Great Rose', its original manager. The stakes were typically five or ten pounds per hundred (usually referred to as a point) but there was also a £100 game. A high-ish score from an afternoon's or evening's bridge might be between 40 and 50 points, which meant that in the £100 game one could win or lose as much as £5,000 in a single session – it was a serious game.

Rebecca's father usually played at TGR's twice a week and he had thought that it might be fun for Tom and Rebecca to watch his play, savour the atmosphere, observe some of the stars of the game, and then join him for a meal. But there was no question of either Tom or Rebecca playing a hand – they were there strictly as kibitzers. Rebecca's father was playing in the ten-pound game and Tom and Rebecca sat silently behind him, one on either side, as he made his bids and played his cards.

Tom was not yet sufficiently qualified to comment on the quality of the play but he was impressed by its sheer speed. Under the rules of the club, they did not play for overtricks and as soon as declarer could see that a contract was certain to be made he would make an immediate declaration. A sure way of ensuring long-term unpopularity, he was told, was to play out a hand in a slow painstaking manner when its success had never been in doubt. The speed of play meant that many more hands were dealt than would normally have been the case. It also meant that it was possible to lose or win more money.

Tom was struck by the contrast between TGR's and the Andrew Robson bridge club, which was the only other bridge club that he had visited. At Robson's a stranger might well have thought that he had stumbled into a rather fashionable Chelsea cocktail party, while at TGR's, the atmosphere resembled that of a more than usually serious meeting of the parochial church council.

Rebecca's father's partner at the bridge table was Boris Schapiro, an irascible legend of the bridge world, whom Tom thought must be very close to his ninetieth birthday. Of the remaining two players at the table, one was a professional and the other an experienced and regular club member. Tom had already observed Zia Mahmood, another bridge superstar, playing at the 'big' £100 table and it was apparent that a significant number of the players were professionals or internationals. As professionals, by definition, made their living from the game, and as bridge was a zero sum game, it was not difficult for Tom to deduce that there must be a number of regular losers who played, to some extent, for the challenge of playing against the very best. He thought that Rebecca's father might well be one of that number.

Tom and Rebecca and her father had a late supper at a small restaurant round the corner from the club in Connaught Street. Talk at the dinner table, inevitably after such an obsessive game, was concentrated on the recent activity at the bridge table. Tom was intrigued by the concept of risk and the law of probabilities. Rebecca's father had posed a question.

'If, as declarer,' he said to Tom, 'you find that four cards of a particular suit are in your opponent's hands, what do you think is the probability of the suit breaking 2–2?'

Tom thought for a moment. 'I would expect the cards to break 2–2 half the time so that the probability is 50 per cent.'

'Wrong,' he was told, 'the probability is only 40 per cent but the probability of the cards breaking 3–1 is 50 per cent.'

Tom found it difficult to follow the logic of this but Rebecca's father had already moved on to finessing technique and the significance of probability in deciding whether, as declarer, to finesse or play for the drop. Tom's head was soon reeling from the string of endless statistics with which Rebecca's father seemed totally familiar. He remembered the catch-question from his childhood – 'if on the spin of a coin it falls "heads" ten times in succession, what are the chances of it falling "heads" for the eleventh time?' The correct answer of 50 per cent seemed against all the odds.

Tom, however, felt a little more comfortable when Rebecca's father suddenly said, 'But never forget human nature. You can study the laws of averages and probabilities until your head explodes but remember that you are still dealing with people. Psychology is also an important element at the bridge table!'

At the end of the meal, after a slight argument as Rebecca's father insisted on paying the bill for all three of them, the discussion led naturally to the subject of etiquette and, of course, to bridge etiquette. 'Nothing is worse at the bridge table,' said Rebecca's father, 'than the gloater. It is bad form to show too much pleasure at a difficult contract achieved, or at a particlarly good play in defence. "Well done, partner" or "bad luck" is enough. It is even rumoured, although the story may well be apocryphal, that a member of the Portland Club, one of the rule-making bodies of the game, was banished from the club for reaching across the table to shake the hand of his partner in congratulation at his success in a particular hand.'

As Rebecca drove Tom back to Parsons Green in her car, his head was still full of the facts and figures from the bridge and dinner tables. But, as his thoughts moved back to the Tudor story, he made a connection. Having observed some of the world's experts on the subject of calculated risk-taking, he now convinced himself that the risks involved in running the Tudor story, although finely balanced, were well worth taking.

The following day Tom marched into the editor's office with his mind made up. He was going to press for immediate publication. He took his editor through the copies of the documents that he had assembled in chronological order. First, he had a copy of the investigating accountants' report – Tudor's prospective expert witness – quantifying Tudor's loss at £10 million. Next, he had a copy of a memorandum from Tudor's solicitors supported by a written opinion from leading counsel testifying to the strength of Tudor's case and its prospects of recovery, which were said to be excellent. Then he had a copy of Mr Justice Templewood's judgement on discovery. Finally, he had a copy of Tudor's press release which stated that Tudor had received £3 million in final settlement of the Palmer litigation.

'The only event that took place between Tudor being advised that there was every reason to believe that they would recover £10 million and its announcement of a settlement of around £3 million, was the judgement on discovery,' said Tom. 'Tudor was fearful of what might be uncovered in the disclosure process, and we know, from the accounting schedules and auditors letters, what that would have been. Although we have no absolute proof, apart from the notes of my interview with Julian Greene, there can be no other explanation. We can, and we must, expose this.'

The editor still looked doubtful but Tom had been persuasive. He looked again at the documents and then back to Tom. 'Let me see an early draft of what you want to say – and stay close to Philip,' a reference to the newspaper's in-house lawyer.

Tom's story appeared in Wednesday's *Financial Times*. It was the first Wednesday in December. The story was flagged in a bold box on the front page of the main paper. The report then dominated the front page of the Companies and Markets section under the headline, 'What does Tudor have to hide?' Tom exposed the cover-up and explained how shareholders had been misled. He catalogued a calendar of events, starting with the announcement of the Palmer acquisition, and leading up to the statement on the settlement of the litigation. He discussed the discovery process and its relevance to the defence's strategy of attacking Tudor's profit record. He speculated on the reasons for Tudor's sudden capitulation in settling for such a modest sum, given the strength of its case. And he concluded that Tudor had not dared to run the risk of having its accounting policies and practices dissected in open court. They had too much to hide.

The magisterial Lex column looked at Tudor in the context of conglomerates as a whole. It returned to the old chestnuts of more disclosure, greater transparency and openness, the complicity of auditors, and the need for vigilant and strong non-executive directors. It was the main business story of the day and it appeared only in the *Financial Times*. It was an important scoop for Tom Curtis.

CHAPTER TWENTY-EIGHT

As Tom Curtis was putting the finishing touches to his article on Tudor, Sarah Armstrong was wending her way home at a time even later than was usual. When she arrived the twins were already sleeping and she crept into their bedroom to kiss the unfurrowed brows of her two little angels. Sarah's working days seemed to get longer and longer and, despite an untold number of well-intentioned resolutions to the contrary, she was seeing less and less of the twins. And when she did see them, her mood was not as sunny and loving as she, and they, would have liked. She was irritable and depressed.

The recovery in the stock market, which she had predicted and anticipated, had failed to happen and the formally high-flying stocks in which RAM was so heavily invested were now well and truly grounded. RAM's funds had continued to under-perform in the second and third quarters of the year and the word 'blip' was no longer in Sarah's or her colleagues' lexicon. She was now dreading the end of the year, which was only a few weeks away; a period of time that included Christmas, which was 'dead' so far as the markets were concerned. There was, therefore, hardly any time for any significant improvement and the likelihood seemed to be that RAM would finish in the bottom dectile of the performance tables.

This was little short of disastrous. Sarah's strong performance in her first three years meant that, taking the four years as a whole, RAM was still in the upper quartile, which, not surprisingly, was how Sarah preferred to present matters. But, equally without surprise, this was not the way things were perceived in the City, where the obsession with the short-term was total. Her competitors could not resist chortling, particularly the value-investors who had now replaced her at the top of the tree. 'RAM fell for the "Bigger Fool Theory",' one of them had been quoted as saying. 'This,' he had explained, 'teaches you to pay too much for something in the belief that someone will come along later and pay more. Well, now the music has stopped and RAM can find nobody on whom it can unload its duff investments.' The press were no longer adoring and RAM's clients, the pension funds, were decidedly restless. But this was not all.

An issue which had now become much more significant was that, not only had the total of the funds under Sarah's control performed poorly, but the results for several individual portfolios within that total were very much worse. The high degree of divergence from the overall average was something that proper risk-management controls should have avoided. But Sarah had stubbornly defended the freedom which RAM managers had to back their own judgement and she had been reluctant to recognise that there was a problem. Now it was too late. One of Sarah's main clients, a blue-chip pension fund, was alleging that RAM had been negligent, was claiming damages, and was threatening legal action if its demands were not met.

Sarah seemed dejected when she joined Simon. She had brushed aside his offer of the usual glass of champagne and said that she would be happy to share with him the bottle of Puligny Montrachet which he had chosen to accompany their poached halibut supper.

'Things no better?' asked a concerned Simon.

'That scheming, greedy bitch at the Oracle Pension Fund suffers from a major personality disorder and she's trying to overcompensate at my expense,' Sarah fumed. 'Three years of out-performance and then just one bad year, and she wants what she describes as "restitution". It's blackmail. She knows that if this gets into the press it will damage our reputation and it will give ideas to other clients.'

'So will you settle?' said Simon.

'That's our dilemma,' said Sarah. 'We dare not settle. First of all, we don't believe that they have a case and that's the opinion of our lawyers. Secondly, if we did seek to arrive at some compromise settlement, simply to keep the client sweet, it would be bound to get out and then we would have a raft of copycat claims. So we are damned if we do, and we are damned if we don't.'

'So what *will* you do?' asked Simon.

'Well, we keep batting it away,' said Sarah. 'Our solicitors have refuted all of their arguments and claims. But they persist. She seems determined to have her day in court and make herself a hero. I just hope that her superiors get some decent legal advice of their own and get her to draw in her horns.'

'Fingers crossed,' said Simon.

'Anyway, it's Christmas in just over two weeks and we are going to have a marvellous time,' he continued, determined to be cheerful. 'The twins are already excited and talking about Father Christmas; how will he find us, and how will he know what to bring, they were asking. I refused to discuss presents and told them that they would just have to wait and see; that Father Christmas would want it to be a surprise. But, over their supper, we did talk about all the arrangements. Your mum and dad on Christmas Day and my parents on Boxing Day. Their eyes were shining and I think that they are really looking forward to it, almost in a grown-up way. And so am I.'

'Good,' said Sarah, 'I am sure it will all be fine and I'm sorry to sound like a killjoy but it has been difficult. And you are right, we will have a marvellous time with the twins. And darling, thank you for buying that really super Christmas tree.'

The following morning Sarah's mood was still gloomy. She was in her office in London Wall by seven o'clock, where she caught up on the overnight news from Wall Street and Tokyo. She then read her *Financial Times*. When her usual meeting with her senior colleagues started at eight o'clock, her blood pressure was already high.

'Have you seen the story about Tudor?' she spat out.

They nodded glumly. Before anybody could offer a more constructive response, one of the dealers put his head round the door.

'Tudor have opened 25 per cent down,' he shouted, before beating a rapid retreat.

One of Sarah's colleagues, the tall, flat-chested girl, then complained, petulantly, 'That company has already cost me almost one per cent in relative performance this quarter alone in my top headline fund.' In each of the last two months Tudor's share price had underperformed the market as a whole, in the eerie way in which bad news is so often anticipated.

Sarah struck the table angrily.

'I've had enough. That bastard Gerald Howard runs Tudor as if he owns the company. Well, we are the largest shareholders in Tudor and we will show him who the real owners are.'

If institutional shareholders have concerns, they never speak directly to the company; they speak to its merchant bank or stockbroker. Sarah had already spoken to James Gordon several times about Tudor's recent poor stock market performance. She now tapped out the numbers for his direct line at Gresham's bank.

James Gordon was beginning to feel the heat. His telephone, despite the early hour, had rung incessantly as institutional shareholders in Tudor wanted to know what on earth was going on. In a discussion with Gerald Howard, James had been unimpressed by Gerald's bluster and by his threats of taking legal action against the *Financial Times*. The call from Sarah Armstrong was, therefore, well timed. James, also, had just about had enough of Gerald Howard. He was quick to interpret her message. She wanted action. And she wanted James Gordon to wield the knife. He was happy to oblige.

James was invariably well pleased with himself but he took particular pleasure in the role he was now about to play in cutting Gerald Howard down to size. The senior of the non-executive directors of Tudor was well known to him, as sat on the boards of a number of other companies that were also clients of Gresham's. James telephoned him and, without sacrificing his normal courtesy and traditional good manners, told him of the shareholder dissatisfaction with Tudor, of their outrage at today's *Financial Times* coverage and, of the need for changes at the top. He conveyed the coded signal that, if he wished to continue to enjoy the goodwill of Gresham's, he should act now.

Tudor's non-executive directors had hitherto been supine. They now acted with surprising speed. The Gresham's nomineee had at last been given some backbone as a result of the ultimatum contained within James's thinly veiled threat to his future livelihood. They had to be seen to be doing something and the easiest thing to do was to fire the chairman, Gerald Howard, which, at a hastily convened board meeting, they proceeded to do. They then, for good measure, threw out the finance director. The fact that not a voice had previously been raised by any of them against any of the policies – accounting or otherwise – pursued by the company over so many years of apparent success was of no account. Cabinet responsibility was not, it seemed, a feature of corporate governance.

Meanwhile, life in the City continued much as before.

CHAPTER TWENTY-NINE

For Gerald Howard, life was now to be very different. He had blotted his copybook and the City would be unforgiving. It subscribed to President Truman's dictum that 'no one ever changes, except maybe for the worse.' Gerald was quickly made to realise that the power and influence which he had enjoyed for so long had been entirely due to his position. And that once that position was lost, he was of no consequence. The speed with which this change took place – the overnight transformation – had about it a cruel brutality. The telephone no longer rang, and the postman rarely called – and when he did it was to deliver bills, junk mail, and the occasional missive from the Inland Revenue. There were no more invitations from banks and City institutions to lunches, grand dinners, and privileged places in corporate boxes.

The Tudor share price, which had been two pounds at the time of the Palmer deal, had continued its downwards drift after Gerald's departure and was now 60p. He had never been a large shareholder, but the small shareholding which he did possess was much reduced in value and his share options were virtually worthless. Despite his superficially generous golden handshake, Gerald was far from being a wealthy man. He would need to find alternative work, but this would not be easy. As a result of institutional and media pressure, there was now a vastly increased demand for squeaky-clean, non-executive directors of so-called independence for quoted companies; and the massive expansion of private equity funds – which was the new name for unadventurous venture capital – had created openings for experienced executives; but the nature of Gerald's departure from Tudor almost certainly ruled him out from both. Things would never be the same again. His twelve years of workaholic effort to please the City had been in vain.

Mark Palmer's prospects were even bleaker. His euphoria at the settlement of his legal action with Tudor had been short-lived. He had been traumatised by the fury and power of Gerald Howard and Tudor, as reflected in their solicitor's letters, and by the advice of his own solicitor with regard to the strength of Tudor's case. It had seemed that he might lose everything. The sudden opportunity to settle for a sum which, although large, was still significantly short of everything, had been an enormous relief. A more sobering reassessment of his finances, however, particularly in the light of the continuing decline in Tudor's share price, had soon reintroduced the demons into his feverish mind.

The £750,000 cash for the settlement had meant further recourse to the banks. The additional borrowings were also secured on the Tudor shares, whose value at the time of the takeover had been £4 million. At the time of the settlement, their value had still been £3,500,000 and the banks had been reasonably comfortable with their security. But with the Tudor share price now 60p, Mark's shareholding was worth only £1,200,000, and, as he was still locked into the restrictions imposed by the purchase agreement, he could not sell. The banks were again pressing for a reduction in his borrowings and his sisters' husbands were adamant that he should not be allowed anywhere near his sisters' money.

He was also now estranged from his third wife. There was no particular trigger that brought about the separation, just a general feeling of discontent and depression, resulting, at least in part, from Mark's business problems and uncertain financial future. And Gail had never forgiven Mark for the loss of their summer holiday. Salt had been rubbed into her wounds when she discovered that Paul and Helen had travelled to Mougins under their own steam and had enjoyed their usual two-week stay, but this time at a local auberge. Unbelievably, she now blamed Paul for their financial catastrophe.

There was a tiny grain of truth in this as the high discounts that Paul had negotiated on behalf of F&G had indirectly led to Nigel Kendal's falsifications. It could be argued that the large volume but low margin F&G orders, which had once seemed to be the lifeline for Palmer's business had, in fact, brought about its downfall. In any event, she had convinced herself that it was all Paul's fault and she would no longer see Helen.

The affair with Jane had fizzled out. And it was very much Jane's doing. Mark had thought that he had been the instigator of the holiday fling but, in retrospect, it had been as much Jane's idea. And while his fling had, for a time, developed into an obsession, for Jane it had simply made her more aware of the opportunities now available to her in her new state of liberation.

Mark was unemployed, and unemployable. He would have to sell his homes. The Porsche had gone and there would be no more trips to St Moritz. The third Thursday in September was the day Mark Palmer's world had fallen apart.

It looked as if his nightmares would continue.

Tom Curtis was the one person to emerge from the Palmer/Tudor imbroglio with his reputation enhanced. But he was not entirely happy. He had been promoted at the *Financial Times* and had a wider role within the newspaper, with a particular brief for in-depth, investigative stories. He was also increasingly to be seen and heard on television and radio news programmes, commenting on City and business issues.

But he was becoming disenchanted with his newspaper. The *Financial Times* had a longstanding and deserved reputation for objectivity. It was *the* journal of record for finance and business. Tom thought that the paper was now putting this reputation at risk by its passionate advocacy of European monetary union. He found its editorial comments in support of Britain's early entry into the single European currency, strident and unquestioning, and he was even more concerned at the extent to which those views were colouring its news reporting. It seemed to Tom only reasonable to have some doubts and reservations on an issue of such magnitude, particularly when the decision, once taken, was irrevocable. Tom's pride in working for the newspaper had been dented and he had a vague feeling of dissatisfaction.

Tom and Rebecca had now moved in together and Tom looked forward to spending more time at home with her. She had taken the opportunity presented by the Tudor public relations disaster to leave her employment and to follow Tom's advice by going into public relations in the book trade. She had teamed up with an old girlfriend, who already worked in publishing, and they had set up in business together. Initially, they were both to work from home but planned to look for offices when they had a sufficient number of clients.

Rebecca was exhilarated by her new opportunity and was getting more satisfaction from her work at a time when Tom's was waning. What Tom really wanted to do, he now thought, was to establish a career as a writer of fiction and to spend less time in the world of business and finance. He was soon to meet his agent, at lunch, where they were to discuss the prospects of getting an advance from a publisher that would be sufficiently large to allow him to give up his full-time work at the *Financial Times*. But he was not optimistic.

CHAPTER THIRTY

The low point of Sarah Armstrong's *annus horribilis* was her appearance in the witness box at the Royal Courts of Justice in the Strand. It had proved to be impossible to achieve an acceptable settlement with the Oracle Pension Fund and the pension fund's manager – Sarah's 'scheming bitch' – had achieved her ambition of 'her day in court'. The media interest was intense as the implications of the case for the whole of the fund-management industry became clear. If Oracle could prove to the court's satisfaction that RAM had been negligent and was in breach of its specific or implied contract, then it would be entitled to damages in compensation for the losses which it had incurred as a result of the fund's under-performance. Oracle was claiming that these losses amounted to more than £50 million. If it was successful, then the trustees of every other pension fund in the land would be examining their own contracts with their fund managers, looking at relative performance, and considering their options. Lawyers were already rubbing their hands in anticipation.

Oracle's case was that its management contract with RAM included clauses that required RAM to manage its portfolio so that the relative performance fell within certain specific parameters. It argued that RAM's controls were so lax that it had failed to meet this requirement; that Sarah had delegated the management of the fund to a portfolio manager who was variously described as a 'wild card', a 'loose cannon' and a 'maverick' or 'rogue' manager. That she had failed to control him or adequately to monitor his performance and that the outcome was a result that was significantly outside the agreed parameters. This, Oracle alleged, had directly led to its loss.

City figures flocked to the law courts to witness – many hoped – the humiliation of Sarah under cross-examination by the ferocious, forensically precise and highly talented QC, who had been retained by Oracle. Some of those who came to the hoped-for feast were her former victims. They were not to be disappointed. What they saw was Sarah's proud demeanour slowly crushed under the hostile, relentless line of questioning from Oracle's counsel. Her answers became longer, more technical, repetitive and eventually rambling. She was repeatedly pressed by the judge to answer questions plainly and simply. At the end of almost a week of cross-examination, she appeared a diminished figure, with her fingers restlessly moving up and down the side of the witness box, and her upper body slumped slightly forward, in striking contrast to her normally severe and upright posture.

The outcome remained in doubt right up until the end. There had been one or two half-hearted attempts to reach an out-of-court settlement as the case had progressed but these had been frustrated because the knock-on consequences of any sizeable payment by RAM were too horrendous to contemplate. And Oracle was determined not to accept a purely nominal offer.

When announcing his decision, the judge was scathing in his condemnation of the lack of proper systems, procedures and controls at RAM. He compared, unfavourably, its unprofessional conduct with the role it sought to play in forming a judgement on the professionalism and competence of those who ran the companies in which it was invested. However, he said that he had formed the view with some reluctance that the management contract was too loosely drawn and that, despite what he described as RAM's lamentable performance, it was not possible to conclude that it had failed to perform within its terms.

It was, for Sarah, a Pyrrhic victory. RAM had got off – but almost on a technicality. Procedures on risk control would be introduced – perhaps even by the dreaded consultants – and management agreements would be more tightly drawn. But Sarah had no appetite for this. She was scarred by her long ordeal in the witness box and her reputation was tarnished. She had been shown to be only human after all, and she was now determined, genuinely, to spend more time with her family.

Simon, in the meantime, stung by a newspaper reference to him in the context of the RAM court case that 'a consultant working from home' is no more than a euphemism for unemployment, had returned to work in the City. Sarah and Simon were now, therefore – for the moment – a more traditional family unit with Sarah looking after the home and the twins. And they still had their millions. But, and on this Sarah was quite certain, she would be back.

CHAPTER THIRTY-ONE

After the settlement Jeremy Stephens heard little from the other participants in the Tudor fiasco. He took a couple of despairing calls from Mark, and Alan Copeland of Chiswells had also telephoned. Alan, with his teflon-coated reputation for risk avoidance still intact, had offered commiserations, shed a few crocodile tears and suggested that perhaps things could have been worse.

Jeremy, in many ways, had suffered most of all from the fallout. He had broken the cardinal rule of his profession – at least by the standards of the profession that existed when Jeremy had been trained by Bill Foster. He had let down his client.

Although Gerald Howard and Mark Palmer had got what he thought were their just desserts, this gave him no cause for satisfaction. He felt that he, and the firm of which he was senior partner, were responsible for the whole débâcle. And he had placed his family and his partners and his partners' families and the whole practice in jeopardy. If Tudor's legal action had achieved the success that at one time had seemed guaranteed, they would all have been ruined. They had been very, very lucky; in the event, they had suffered no financial loss.

Despite the protestations of his partners, Jeremy had taken early retirement. He had lost his self-confidence and no longer thought that he could do justice to his clients' interests. And although previously he had looked forward to retirement, he was now at a loss. He did not know what he was going to do. He could play more golf and perhaps improve his handicap; he had joined the board of a former client company as a non-executive director and its chairman was hoping that Jeremy could help them with their strategic planning. But that was not going to be enough.

He had been offered an office to use as a base at Stephens Foster, but had not felt comfortable at the prospect of going back to his old firm each day. His recent resignation as the chairman of his local Liberal Democrats had taken away what could have been a potential retirement activity. And he no longer had the solace of his London club.

Jeremy had never really seen himself as a clubbable man. He had found the Pall Mall and St James's clubs of his acquaintance stuffy, smug and uninviting. On his occasional visits, as a guest, to the Garrick, he had found most of its members generally too pleased with themselves and had thought that the tie said it all. Then one of his clients had introduced him to a club a little removed from the habitat of traditional clubland, in the West End of London.

Burke's Club had a small and friendly membership. Jeremy had taken to it and had become a member. On a rare occasion he would take a client to lunch at a side table. But most often, he would lunch at the long, central table where he would meet people of different backgrounds and where they would put the world to rights over a shared bottle of wine. He had been determined to use the club more often on his retirement, when he naturally expected to have more time.

But the club had recently been infected by the contagion of political correctness. Burke's was a men's club, and the facilities for the entertainment of women, either as guests of members or as guests at private functions, were strictly limited. The club secretary had stated that, for this reason, it was now becoming difficult to negotiate reciprocal arrangements with American clubs. At the same time, a number of members had expressed the wish to dine at the club with their spouses or other female friends. Treating the club more as a restaurant, thought Jeremy, at exactly the time when London had an abundance of restaurants of good quality but few clubs of character. He was fearful that changes which had not been properly thought through, and which would be irrevocable, might damage what he saw as the club's unique ambience.

172

A meeting of members was held to discuss the issue. The voting was close. Initially, it was thought that the motion – to offer dining facilities to lady guests (as they were described) – had been carried. Despite the fact that there was only one vote difference, a recount had been refused. Then it was discovered that there had been a mistake in the manner in which abstentions had been dealt with in the calculations. On a reappraisal, it was found that the resolution had, in fact, been lost. Now it was ordered that the recount that had previously been denied should be carried out. In the chaos and confusion that reigned, it was again declared that the motion was carried – again by a single vote. Jeremy had resigned in disgust – as much with the incompetence as with the principle.

The chain of events that led to Jeremy's decision to leave the political party, which he had actively supported for more than 40 years, since Suez, could he said to have started at the adoption meeting and his subsequent letter to the party leader. Despite several reminders, he had, to his growing irritation, received no reply to his letter.

Shortly after his latest reminder, by chance, Jeremy had cause to visit the party headquarters in Cowley Street. It was in connection with a routine administrative matter to do with the financial support for key constituencies. Normally this was something which would have been handled by the local treasurer, but Jeremy got a buzz from his infrequent visits to Cowley Street and, with the time now available from the luxury of his retirement, he had offered to act as messenger.

As Jeremy descended the Cowley Street staircase on his way to the front hall, having dealt with the minor item of business, he was surprised to see, through an open office doorway, the party leader talking to what Jeremy assumed to be a member of the staff. Jeremy automatically half-raised his hand in greeting, which provoked a similar guarded and hesitant response, before Jamie Kilkenny resumed his interrupted conversation.

Jeremy had been taken a little aback by the surprise of the accidental, almost confrontation, but that was as nothing compared to his shock at the leader's appearance. Dressed in a sweatshirt, faded jeans and scruffy trainers, he looked as if he might have just disembarked from the overnight sleeper from Scotland. Jeremy, while recognising that he might well be considered an old-fashioned traditionalist, felt that standards were important and that this was an inappropriate way for the party leader to appear at the party's offices on party business.

Before returning home, Jeremy took a long, slow, disconsolate and meandering walk through St James's Park. There was no reason to believe that Jamie Kilkenny had recognised Jeremy in that fleeting moment in Cowley Street. And even if he had, he would not necessarily have made the connection with the letter, which he might not even have seen or read. Nonetheless, Jeremy had found the brief encounter to be unsettling. And the cumulative effect was beginning to tell. Now, not only did he have concerns about party policy, but also about the leader.

When Jeremy arrived home, he decided to write a final reminder letter to the party leader's office at the House of Commons. Seven days later there had still been no acknowledgement of any kind. Now Jeremy had had enough. This, what he considered to be an astonishing discourtesy, a lack of ordinary, straightforward good manners, was the last straw. If, he thought, the party leader cannot be bothered to respond to a senior member of his party, then what chance do ordinary people have? He resigned from his position as chairman of the constituency party and said that he would not be renewing his party membership.

Jeremy felt humiliated and drained by the trauma that was involved in his decision. He had been brought up as a Catholic, had, for as long as he could remember, supported the same football team, banked at Barclays – and voted Liberal. They had all seemed to go together. They were part of his life. Had been tribal. He had never before thought of changing any of these lifelong and comforting arrangements. And although, even now, he could not quite contemplate voting for any other party, his resignation as a member of the Liberal Democrats felt like a bereavement.

Jeremy had never considered himself as a resigner or a quitter, and had never been one for bold gestures. But now, within the space of a year, he had lost two of his main outside interests. Interests that he had hoped to develop in retirement. However, although this was clearly a blow – particularly the political involvement, which he would sorely miss – they had never been more than peripheral activities. Jeremy's whole life had been devoted to the practice. For nearly 40 years Stephens Foster had been his life. He was now finding it difficult to adjust.

As he continued to reflect, sitting alone in his study at home, he searched his mind for some long-lost quotation that seemed to him to be particularly relevant. And then he remembered, of course, it was Enoch Powell. He took Brewer's political dictionary from his bookshelf and soon found the reference.

'All political lives, unless they are cut-off in mid-stream at a happy juncture, end in failure, because that is the nature of politics and of human affairs'.

It seemed to Jeremy to be relevant to more than just political lives – to be as appropriate a comment on business and professional careers – and perhaps on life itself. Because few people actually achieve what they really believe that they are capable of achieving. And therefore, he mused, if only in the light of their own best expectations, most might consider that they have failed.

As Jeremy continued thumbing through the book, his eye caught a quotation from Theodore Roosevelt. 'It is hard to fail, but it is harder still never to have tried to succeed.' That sounded better.